A CIVIL WAR WITHIN

ETHAN FRECHETTE

To Ezra Joel, I love you with all my heart. Learn from my life and my mistakes. Be better than me. Be better than everyone who comes before you, and break the cycle that holds so many of us hostage to suffering.

Preface

Identity is a very touchy subject in our modern time, and rightfully so. It's something that we all thoughtfully search for yet very few of us ever truly grasp. Our true identity is elusive, wrapped up in expectations formed by society and others instead of our own experiences. This is especially true for members of the younger generation in America, who are trying to find where they belong not only in society but also in the grand scheme of history. For young men in particular, it is a very confusing time, as what society considers masculine is constantly in flux, ever changing to fit what is popular. "Man up" and "suck it up" have become our mantras, the masks we wear to show our masculinity while our true, unique, and beautiful identities slip beyond the periphery of our vision.

Working in oncology and various other areas of the medical field as a nurse, I have become very comfortable with conversations about death. Fortunately and unfortunately, death has become an almost-constant part of my life. A daily reminder of impermanence and the fact that my actions are my only true belongings—everything else is just fleeting junk that accumulates over time. In the exam and infusion rooms with suffering men and women, I have encountered patients who have accepted they are about to leave this life and go into the next one. On several occasions, I have been privileged to be at the bedside of people taking that last leap toward eternity. There is something very profound about being with someone as they pass away, as their physical existence is washed away like an ocean tide washing a sandcastle off the beach. Though the sand is no longer a castle, you know that the sand still exists and is a part of that beautiful beach.

Many times I have felt as if I could see every decision they had ever made wash over their face in one blissful second as they took their last breath. Countless years of memories wiped clean, leaving behind an empty, rigid shell. It is both heartbreaking and beautiful to watch, and it always surprises me in the end. The individuals who shocked me the most were the ones who had accepted their fate, oftentimes welcoming death as if it were an old friend reunited at last. They stood at the mountaintop of life and gained clarity, able to see the horizon behind them and the journey ahead. It took me so long to understand how someone could accept death like that, because, if I'm being honest, death is one of my biggest fears. It terrifies me that a life of joy, beauty, pain, and struggle can amount to a single breath at the end of the road.

It terrifies me that my entire identity could be washed away in an instant. More than anything, it terrifies me that after all my hard work, I will just leave it all behind. Everyone I love and everything I have struggled for will all be left behind. Ironically, though, I came to realize that these individuals were able to accept death because they truly understood who they were—they knew their identity was so much more than just a physical body, more than just what they could see and touch.

We often associate our identity with who we are on the outside: how we look, the clothes we wear, the house we live in, the tech we have. When we die, and the physical washes away just like a sandcastle, there is no physical identity left for those who loved us. Yet that doesn't mean there isn't anything left, that there isn't beauty left for the world to see.

I remember one gentleman in particular named Richard. Before I became a nurse, I was a caregiver at a nursing home, and I took care of Richard and his wife, Ruth. I had gotten very close to him and his family, but it wasn't long before things started to go downhill for Richard. His wife was diagnosed with Lewy body dementia and would often forget who Richard was. Several times a week, Richard would come out in the hall, weeping, while Ruth could be heard screaming in the background. His wife would forget they were married and would wake up and attack Richard, thinking he was a stranger. Richard's heart broke. After Ruth passed away, Richard became very depressed and lonely. He often would flirt with the female caregivers in hopes of finding some companionship and comfort. He also blamed everyone for his depression and the unfortunate events that had happened to him. He blamed the doctors, the nurses, even his long-deceased father. Every decision he made, every negative comment or behavior, was someone else's fault. Richard was surely in a tough situation, but he was letting his circumstances dictate who he was and control his entire being. Richard was no longer sweet, gentle, and loving. Through his struggles, Richard lost his identity. He became a stranger to himself. He forgot who Richard was. I remember during the last week of his life, Richard recapped his life and the decisions he had made. He told me about his adventures in World War II where he'd been a plane engineer. He reminisced about how he met his beautiful wife in Bible college. He spent hours telling wonderful stories, and I eagerly listened, hoping to siphon some wisdom off the old man. Every struggle, every pain, every romance over ninety years was listed one by one. I expected depression would follow such a retelling of his life, given the ending was not "happily ever after." After all, there he was, sitting in a room, letting strangers bathe him after his wife had died forgetting she ever knew him. But something was different. I noticed Richard started to break the cycle. I watched as every story told brought clarity to his depression and loneliness. The sadness was slowly being wiped away as he told me these stories. As he took ownership and realized that he wasn't defined by the circumstances he found himself in, he became "lighter," as if air had rushed into the room and he was able to breathe again.

I'll never forget what he said after he finished his final story, which was about the last year he spent with Ruth. He looked at me and said, "Ethan, I lived a good, hard life, and I am happy to die knowing I made a name for myself. I know that I am a good man!" The following week, Richard passed away.

I tell Richard's story for two reasons. One, it shows the magic of storytelling and the power storytelling has not just on ourselves but on others too. The stories that Richard told me have forever changed me. Two, Richard's story addresses the age-old question, who am I? I believe that everyone in our society struggles with that question now more than ever. Society has a lot of opinions about who we should and shouldn't be. Depending on where you stand on the political spectrum, the opinions change. If you are a man who falls on the liberal side, you are automatically expected to subscribe to BuzzFeed, have a big beard, and have a large following on Instagram. If you fall into the conservative category, men are meant to be Ron Swansons, never having emotion and never apologizing for anything. Now, these are obviously comical generalizations, but they are meant to show that our identity is largely defined by our society and politics. Should that be the case? The world tells young men who are fierce and courageous to be prim and proper. Young men who are shy and timid are told to be more outgoing and confident. The truth is there is no singular identity for anyone. We all grow up with unique circumstances, making our own choices and facing the outcomes. The only thing that is true for every person (all humans, no matter how you identify) is we should be fighting every day to love one another, end suffering, and make our community better. That only happens when everyone is fighting for their unique identity and living passionately.

We must break the cycle that keeps us tied to our past and perpetuates our pain and suffering. When we break that cycle and choose to fight to find who we are, we are declaring a civil war within. We are declaring war against the negative cycles that keep us suffering—cycles like blaming others for our mistakes, constantly hating our bodies, feeling stupid, feeling alone, feeling weird. Whatever negative cycle you keep playing in your head, it is time to break it and find out how beautiful, powerful, and unique you truly are. As my wife's favorite show so accurately states, "Demons run when a good man goes to war."

I told Richard's story because, when faced with death, he chose to enter that fight, that civil war within. Richard had been spiraling down a dark hole because the circumstances of his life had gotten too heavy to bear, and I can't blame him for that. A disease had taken his wife's memories and left Richard alone. Yet in the last week of his life, he broke free of any power the past had over him. He didn't tell me, "It is all the doctors' fault my wife isn't here anymore." Nor did he say, "I lost my wife. I hate my life, and I am lonely." No, he looked back on his life and saw his identity wasn't wrapped up in his current circumstances. Richard had lived an amazing life. When his loved ones look back on his life, they will remember Richard as a faithful husband, a funny uncle, and a loving father, not the decrepit physical form that left this world. You see, when the idea of impermanence became clear, so did Richard's true identity. He chose to go to war with his heart and the depression and anger.

He chose to leave the world the way he lived, happy. Richard broke the cycle and died free from suffering.

I want to die as Richard did in my old age. That is why death scares me so much. It has nothing to do with fear of what is next. My fear lies in the people I leave behind. But if we are able to answer this intimately personal question, who am I? then what is there to fear? In the end, I want to look at all the decisions I've made and all the pain life has given me and realize that I lived a good life and I am happy to die knowing I am a good man.

This book is not a step-by-step instruction manual on how to find your identity as a man. It is not a guide on how to choose war over passivism or vice versa. Any institution, be it church or society in general, that gives you a cookie-cutter example of who you are is simply wrong. This book isn't even a self-help book; it's a story. Some of humanity's greatest lessons were delivered through stories passed on through generations. The only true event in this book is that of the battle I am fighting in my own heart. The main character, Ezra, is a fourteen-year-old boy named after my son, but the struggles that he goes through—dealing with bullies, his self-image, and his relationship with his father—are the ones I dealt with when I was fourteen. That was all stuff that I had to work through, and an event like the one in this story happened in my life, but unfortunately it took a lot longer than fourteen years for me to understand the truths I talk about. However, I am grateful for all the struggles I have had over my brief time on this earth thus far because I am very confident that I know who I am.

This story is the kicking-off point for these young men in their journey to find their unique identity. They won't end their journey having the answer to the question, who am I? But they will know where to start going, and hopefully you, as the reader, will too. This book started as a story I was writing to my son before he was even born. In the United States, we aren't very good at shepherding our children into adulthood like other cultures, so I wanted to give my son a story that symbolized a "coming-of-age ceremony" that explains the lessons I have learned in my life about letting go and breaking the cycle of suffering. It quickly turned into a full-length book. I hope that everyone who reads this book can relate to the characters and can grasp the struggles these young men are facing to find their true identity.

The last thing I want to say to my reader is this: Fight. Don't settle. Don't let the world tell you who you are. Don't let anyone tell you who you are. Reclaim your identity. Trust your gut. There is something inside of us all that is hungry for truth, hungry for more, and desperate to rage against the expectations that are put before us. You are so much more than your past. You are so much more than your anger. You are so much more than your failures. You are so much more than any sexual or physical abuse you may have endured. You are a fighter. So fight!

Chapter I
The Great Unknown

I am standing in front of an army of a thousand men. I know nothing about them or where they came from. I look for somewhere to hide, for something that will conceal me from this vast army, but everywhere I look is just dirt—nothing living. Two things I know for sure: I am alone, and I am terrified. I stand hopelessly alone in the Valley of Fire. How can I possibly fight all these men? What if I am too weak? What if I fail? What if, what if, what if? My heart beats faster and faster to the sound of war drums ... BUMP, BUMP ... BUMP, BUMP ... BUMP, BUMP. And then it starts. The vast army starts its descent down the dirt-covered hill toward me. All I can see is a massive black wave moving toward me through a great cloud of dust and rubble. Again I look for somewhere to run yet find nothing. I know in that moment that I must fight. I take a symbolic step forward, clearing my mind of distractions. I grab a handful of dirt and let it fall between my fingers as if letting the wind carry away my fear. I begin to count the seconds as the army moves closer and closer. Five. Four. I take my stance and broaden my shoulders. Three. I draw my sword. Two. One. I spit on the ground and brace myself for battle. Zero. With eyes closed, I grip my sword, my knuckles white, and swing away at my enemy, but fear prevents my eyes from opening. I can hear the cries of war. Yet when I finally open my eyes ... I am awake.

Wait, what? I wake up now? I mean, come on, that was the best part of the dream.

I lay back down and forced my eyes shut in hopes that I would find myself in the dream once more. It reminded me of when my dad let me watch *Independence Day* but made me close my eyes when the squid-looking alien thing started talking with its hissing voice. I mean, come on, those were the best parts! I rolled onto my side, put the pillow over my head, and squeezed my eyes shut again, giving it one last shot, but it was no use. All I could focus on was the smell of bacon from the kitchen. So I reluctantly pulled the covers off, threw the pillow across the room in disappointment, and forced myself out of bed. I walked to the bathroom and went through the joyous routine of getting ready for the day (I am saying that with sarcasm, by the way).

I finished putting on my pants, styling my hair, and brushing my teeth and found myself bored with it all. Something just seemed missing every morning. The routine of getting ready so that I could look good felt empty. Plus, it didn't matter how much work I put in or what new hair product or clothes I got. No matter how much I stared in the mirror, I never liked what I saw. Despite my dissatisfaction, though, I pressed on. I headed to the kitchen to find my epic battle's great reward of bacon and pancakes.

My mother, as usual, came over and kissed me good morning, and I kissed her back reluctantly, as if showing my mother affection was something to be ashamed of.

"Good morning, Ezra. How did my handsome little boy sleep?"

She was always calling me things like *cute* and *adorable* and proceeded to mess up my hair by trying to rub all the hairspray out of it (my hair is a no-touch zone, by the way; whatever good looks and charm I may have come from my well-styled hair). Then entered my father, who proceeded to chuckle at my expense, as usual, as he watched my mom mess with me. He made his daily comment of "You are going to go bald early, Ezra, if you keep putting all that crap in your hair." He continued, "It's like our son is Michael Jackson or something." Ha-ha, so funny, Dad, haven't heard you say that one before. Oh wait, you forgot "Don't get too close to the stove, son. Your hair might set on fire." Or his usual favorite question: "When did our son become so gay?" But like most mornings, I just shrugged his comments off and moved on, knowing it was not worth arguing about.

I devoured every piece of meat and fluffy goodness

within minutes of the food hitting my plate. You would have sworn my nightmare was more than just a dream and that I had just finished a day's worth of battle.

"You planning to work out with me today, Ezra? It's biceps and triceps. I'll make a man of you yet," my dad asked with a smirk, then chuckled to himself, knowing my answer was already a no.

It wasn't that I didn't enjoy working out. I just didn't know how to explain to a workout junkie like my dad, who was always pushing me to lose more weight, that I always felt worse about myself when I worked out with him. There I would be, huffing and puffing, my untoned body jiggling at every movement, while he stood there acting like he never struggled with his weight in his life. So of course, my answer was a no.

"I think I am going to take a rain check, Dad. Plus, don't we have someplace to be, anyway?" I asked, excited that my excuse was one already laid out for me.

My parents had signed me up for a "Young Men's Summer Camping Trip" (they weren't very creative with the name there) in the Valley of Fire. Sounded intense! I was not a huge camper, to be honest; I was raised a city kid. I enjoyed living in Las Vegas and having access to everything twenty-four hours a day, seven days a week. I knew I wasn't old enough to do many things, but I definitely liked having the option. Who doesn't like being able to get Sonic tater tots at one a.m.?

Anyway, we were going camping with this guy who had a really odd name that I still had no idea how to say: Vivek. Who named their kid Vivek? Whatever. So yeah, this guy named Vivek was the leader of a young men's mentorship program, and every six months he took a new group of guys out camping. He always went to the Valley of Fire. Supposedly Vivek said this was because "the name matches the heart of a man." I was not sure what that meant, and it sounded kind of creepy, to be honest. My parents thought I should go on this trip to work on my "self-esteem problems." It seemed like all of my friends who went came back with a new attitude on life. They came back ... *old*, for lack of a better word. All they talked about now was their futures and what they wanted to do with their lives. They talked about being a man, "breaking the cycle of suffering," and "changing the world for the better." Some of them were talking about marriage already and how they wanted to become "better men" so they could "better lead their future families." I wasn't even fifteen years old yet. I didn't have any desire to have a full-time girlfriend yet, let alone a family.

I couldn't help but wonder why my parents were doing this, though. Why did they want me to grow up so fast? I was only fourteen years old, and it was summer. I should be doing stupid things with my friends, meeting girls, and having fun. Being young, wild, and free, right? My focus should be on who I should go out with on Friday and what sport I should play next. I was not ready to be old yet or to focus on the hard parts of life. I wanted to go out and have fun, not sit around and make lame dad jokes. Every time I told my dad I was hungry, he would reply, "Hi, Hungry, what happened to Ezra?" I didn't know if I was ready for that kind of future for myself.

My friends Jordan and Daniel were coming on the camping trip too. Daniel was even missing a party he had been planning to go to on Friday just because his mother was making him go on this trip. It seemed a little fishy to me, you know? Something wasn't adding up, but hell, I would have done anything to get out of the house for a few days. Being fourteen in Nevada during the summer means sitting inside all day, watching *CSI: Las Vegas* reruns, and laughing while asking yourself, Why is it that every room in a show based out of the City of Lights is so dimly lit? The summer in Las Vegas is too hot to enjoy doing much else.

Anything would've been an improvement on my day. And so off we went to the great unknown.

Chapter 2
Find Your Name

My parents dropped me off in the parking lot of my high school and said good-bye. It was a really strange moment, especially if you ever saw my high school. It was situated basically in the middle of a massive flat dirt lot with about two to three miles of nothing in either direction. The school's name was Sierra Vista, which was Spanish for "Mountain View." I always found this ironic because the only "mountains" nearby were dirt hills, most of which were man-made, and I could see right over them if I hiked up them for more than a minute. The school looked more or less like a prison. Not the destination you expected to be dropped off by your parents on a hot summer day when there was no school in session.

Reluctantly, though, I got out of the car, and they handed me my sleeping bag and pillow. Then my dad said, "I hope you know how proud I am of you, son. You are a good man." I found that to be the oddest

moment of all—my dad had never called me a man
before. And I had done nothing to earn such a title.
Despite the oddity of his words, something seemed so
intimate about that moment. My mother, on the other
hand, kissed me on the forehead and just started crying.
I could barely understand what she was saying under her
sobbing, but it sounded something like, "I love you so
much. I can't wait to meet my young man after all this."

After that I was convinced this Vivek guy was taking
us to the Valley of Fire to burn us. This trip just got a
whole lot creepier. But there I was anyway, eagerly
waiting to meet Vivek. After my buddies had arrived and
shared similar stories of awkward, unprovoked intimacy
with their parents, we all started talking about who we
pictured this Vivek guy to be. We thought he was going
to be some old guy with long silver hair and probably
black nose hairs popping out. I was sure he was going to
be missing a bunch of teeth and was going to have a big
potbelly. We didn't know what to expect. Vivek just
sounded like he was going to be a hippie version of
Santa Claus. I mean, it made sense. He was taking us
into the desert to get all "kumbaya," and we sure as hell
had never met the guy. Everything about this trip was as
mysterious as Santa.

As Daniel, Jordan, and I stood there waiting for
Hippie Claus, a guy my father's age maybe, in his
midthirties, came walking up to us with Connor, the
counselor from the winter camp that we all went to this
past year. The man with Connor was pretty tall, and he
looked right at me with his huge blue eyes, almost like

he could see right through me. I don't know how to describe it, but when this guy looked at me, I felt like he was calling something out of me, something very angry. Something painful. I felt like that little boy in my nightmare standing terrified of what lay before me. It was safe to say this guy scared me, but not because he was intimidating—the exact opposite, actually. Despite his intense glare, this man was very comforting in his appearance. He was an intersection of two parallels: intimately welcoming and mysteriously off-putting.

This whole time that this guy and I were staring at each other, Connor was talking about "unique masculinity," "identity," and how it was time to find our "name." It was clear that I missed a few things he said because the idea of finding my name sounded like a very silly concept. My name was Ezra; what was there to find? The intense glare of this stranger had captivated my attention. Something in me was drawn to him as if he held a piece of me that I didn't know I was looking for. And though it was clearly weird that we found ourselves staring at each other, I felt excited for the first time about this trip.

Connor kept talking and talking, and finally, he introduced this stranger to us. "This gentleman right here is the director of the young men's mentorship program here in Vegas. We met a long time ago in Israel, and we have been best friends since. I want to introduce you to Vivek."

My buddies looked at me like I knew something they didn't. "Israel?" they both asked me, but I just shrugged my shoulders. I knew just as much as they did.

Vivek stuck his hand out to shake ours. "Gentlemen, I am honored to meet you. I hope you guys are ready because this is not going to be what you are expecting," he said with a crooked smile. He appeared to be getting enjoyment out of our bewilderment. "The next couple of days are not going to be easy on you," he continued. "I am planning to push you and challenge you as men. This trip is designed to help you find your name, your unique identity as a man. Society gives us all cookie-cutter molds to fit into, and most of us go into the mold not knowing anything different. I partnered with Connor here because we want to help you find freedom in your name, in your identity. Freedom in knowing who you truly are. Nothing is more freeing than knowing you are safe within yourself. This winter when you were in camp with Connor, he noted that you three men were ready to take this step to finding your unique identity. Each one of you came to Connor wanting to break the cycle of pain and suffering in your life, wanting to go to war with yourself and become a better version of yourself. This trip is going to help you do that."

I found myself chuckling. This must be some kind of joke. I couldn't understand what this trip would mean to me. When I'd gone to Connor, I had been upset because I struggled with the image of myself—I hated what I woke up to in the morning. How could camping next to a fire and simmering in my own body odor for a few days help my self-esteem? It seemed like Vivek was giving himself a little too much credit.

"Ezra," Vivek said loudly, turning to me as I chuckled. "What does your name mean?"

"I have no idea. Some guy from the Bible?" I said, laughing as if my answer was a witty comeback.

Vivek shook his head with a soft grin, moving past my stupid reply. "Daniel! Jordan! What do your names mean?"

They shrugged. It was clear that we had a lot of work to do to "find our name." Our understanding of who we were at that given moment was just letters on a page. The names Ezra, Daniel, and Jordan only served a purpose for roll call in the classroom or when our parents were calling us to do something. The idea that this stranger could offer anything more seemed far-fetched. Yet something in all of us hoped we were wrong. We hoped that there was more to our names than just letter after letter. Vivek was a nice, a welcoming man, but his intense glare frightened us. Yet it also gave us hope. Hope that there was more to us than just the cookie-cutter mold and fear that we might be too weak to find out what it was. All of these thoughts raced through our minds in a matter of seconds, but it was clear to Vivek that he had our curiosity. Connor and Vivek looked at each other and laughed as if they had just shared some inside joke, like our confusion was familiar to them. Then Vivek walked over to the van, opened the door, and said, "It's time to go, guys. Grab your stuff."

Chapter 3
Why Do You Fight?

We left our school and drove for about two hours. By the time we reached our destination, it was nighttime. We got everything out of the car, and to our surprise, there was no tent to be found. None of us being campers, we decided not to say anything and go with the flow, assuming this must be the normal. As we unrolled our sleeping bags, Vivek got the fire ready by dousing it with lighter fluid. The childlike grin on his face gave me chills, convincing me even more that he was in fact taking us out here to burn us alive. Once the fire settled to a calm roar and we saw that we were safe, we all sat down and passed around some snacks: the typical teenage-boy feast, Cheez-Its and beef jerky. Then Vivek drew our attention to him.

"Do any of you have any idea why I brought you here—why I chose the Valley of Fire?" Vivek asked.

Daniel eagerly raised his hand, always trying to win the affection of anyone who could possibly come across as a father figure. Daniel's father had bailed early in his life, so he was raised by his mom. It made Daniel kind of an overachiever in just about everything. He was a popular kid in school—captain of the football team, a star on the debate team, and the teachers' favorite. Daniel was a smart and talented guy, but he also came across as kind of annoying when he had to fight for attention all the time.

"Yes, Daniel?"

"You brought us here so we can wander through the desert like our ancestors ... like cavemen discovering fire." He stopped and looked around. "Discovering our fire," he said, then grunted and pounded his chest, pretending to be a caveman.

Vivek chuckled. "No, that's not it, but I like the performance, Daniel. Have you ever given thought to joining our theater team?" He looked to me and Jordan. "Anyone else got a guess?"

Jordan whispered something.

"What was that, Jordan? Speak up."

"I said, 'So no one can hear us scream,'" Jordan repeated himself.

Vivek let out an awkward laugh in hopes of making a serious fear seem humorous. "Moving on ... Ezra, what do you think? Why the Valley of Fire?"

"To be honest, I've got nothing for you," I replied.

Vivek didn't laugh this time. In fact, he seemed excited by my answer, like I had just told him what he wanted to hear. He jumped to his feet. "That is exactly right, Ezra. You have nothing. Right now the three of you have nothing. You are just young enough to not be completely jaded by this screwed-up world. You are young enough that your bad habits aren't fully formed, and you can easily be shaped. You have a chance to be better than those before you, to learn from the mistakes of others. I chose the Valley of Fire because that"—he motioned to the campfire in front of us—"is what you will leave here with. You come with nothing but leave with fire."

I wanted his words to be true. I thought back to that recurring nightmare, standing paralyzed with fear before that army. How I would have loved to have "fire" in that moment, but that was just a dream. The reality was I was just some kid living in Sin City who couldn't even face himself in the mirror. The closest thing I got to having fire in me was the summer heat. Life just wasn't theatrical enough to walk around identifying with something like fire. I wanted Vivek's words to be true, but they seemed to fall short.

I think Vivek could tell from the look on my face that I was struggling to understand his theatrical view of life. Oddly enough, he didn't seem bothered by that, but it was clear he wasn't going to give up on me. He sat across the fire with a big grin on his face and asked, "Ezra, have you ever been in a battle?"

"Well, seeing that I am fourteen, no, I haven't, Vivek. Have you?" I responded, slightly irritated by the obvious stupidity of the question.

"Actually, Ezra, yeah, almost every day. I battle against myself. It doesn't have to be physical to still be a battle. I fight against anger for stupid things I have done in the past. Have you ever dreamt of battle, of fighting, Ezra?"

How did he know about my dream? I hadn't told anyone about that, and honestly, I was pretty embarrassed to be having such childish dreams, so I definitely wasn't sharing them with a stranger. Yet somehow, this guy knew about them.

"What are you getting at, man? I am tired and hungry, and I don't want to play your stupid game," I responded in confusion.

Vivek nodded. "Fair enough, Ezra. Men aren't very good at playing mind games. So be honest with me. Each of you went to your camp counselor Connor this past winter with some kind of struggle you were having. Ezra, you are fighting self-esteem issues. Daniel, you are fighting issues with your father never being there. And, Jordan, you are fighting issues with your parents considering divorce—they are still in couples' counseling, right?"

Jordan nodded while looking at the ground.

"Each of you went to Connor with these issues not only to talk but you also expressed a desire to change. You wanted to fight for something better. Most kids just come into his office, talk, then walk out, but you three wanted to fight for a better tomorrow, for a better you. I want to help you three find out why you made the decision to fight. So, I want to ask all of you the question, Why do you fight? I also want to know why you feel ashamed to answer that question."

I didn't know the answer to his question. I sat there puzzled. Every time he asked me about battles or fighting, I wanted to get up and attack. Why was I so defensive over a question like that? It felt like he was challenging me, yet in reality, all he was doing was asking me a simple question: Why do I fight? I know it only took me a second to give him some sarcastic reply, but it felt like a lifetime of thinking.

"How the hell should I know, Vivek? You tell me."

He looked at me and smiled. "I would love to, Ezra. But first, get some sleep." And with that, we all settled into our sleeping bags, feeling confused and bewildered by the conversation that had just taken place. I laid my head down and tried to fall asleep, but Vivek's words kept echoing through my mind.

Chapter 4
Peaceful Chaos

Why do you fight, Ezra?

What does that mean? I asked myself over and over
again. Why had I been so defensive? I curled into my
sleeping bag so that only my head was popping out and
looked up at the sky as if searching for the answer.
There was something so peaceful about all the chaos in
the sky. We were far enough from the city that I could
see the Milky Way galaxy. Every couple of seconds, a
shooting star streaked across the sky like a speeding
missile. Time seemed to stop in those moments I stared
at the dark navy-blue sky. I couldn't hear the roar of the
city anymore, but the roar of nature seemed so much
louder. A coyote howled in the distance, and I could
hear the rippets of frogs nearby. The hum of the cicadas
had calmed to almost a constant lullaby. The gentle
whistle of the wind across the empty floor of the desert
sounded like a muted ocean. The world I was
accustomed to was so far from this place, yet somehow

my heart felt at home.

When sleep finally came, I was immediately carried away to my familiar dream. I found myself standing alone in a desert again, facing a sea of violence. I had never been in a real battle, but the exhaustion I felt when waking up from that nightmare sure as hell made me feel like I had been. I thought about how scared I felt in that dream, how hopeless. When Vivek had asked me why I was ashamed to answer his question, I knew it was because dreams of a battle were childish, right? Just a product of playing too many violent video games or having too much "pent-up energy." I was embarrassed. Even standing up for yourself, fighting for the right reasons, was seen as being an undisciplined child nowadays.

My whole life I had always been on the heavier side. Now that I was a little taller, I came across more muscular than fat, but in sixth grade, that was not the case. Being fat and having asthma, I was terrified of going to PE class. Our PE coach would have us run laps, and if anyone didn't finish in time, we would all have to run another lap. I didn't know my teacher well; maybe he had good intentions and was trying to give us motivation to become healthier and finish in time. But I never finished in time. Four or five of the other kids were getting sick of running extra laps because of me, so they decided to give me a different kind of motivation. Several times a week, they would push me down in the field and kick me around.

They quickly saw they were leaving obvious bruises

on me, so they came up with a new plan. They would bring extra tube socks to PE with them and started putting tennis balls inside them. They would hit me with those so that when I went to "snitch" on them, I couldn't prove anything since the tennis balls were soft enough not to leave any marks. They would lift my shirt up and push me around so my fat would jiggle, calling me names like Chunk from *The Goonies.* They would also laugh and yell "fat pig" over and over, all while the coach watched from a distance. I tried to rationalize why he allowed their abuse to continue. Maybe he had good intentions and was hoping it would motivate me to live healthier, but looking back, it just made me hate my body even more. The first couple of times it happened, I cried and begged them to stop, but soon I just got used to the routine. I tried everything to make it stop. I reported the behavior to my other teachers and did something called peer mediation, where you sit down with another student and talk about it. But with nothing to back up my end of things, it just became a back-and-forth argument, with one person blaming the other over and over. I even tried to run faster, but all the abuse didn't change the underlying fact that I was actually fat and out of shape. Nothing changed. I could try to run faster but just found myself having another asthma attack, puffing on my inhaler, gasping for air, a quarter of the way into it.

My dad was the only one with true intentions. He listened and tried to teach me how to box and tried to get me to work out to make things easier in PE, but my warped self-image just started making me see everyone as a bully, even my dad, who just wanted to help. With my dad's generational, ignorant jokes, calling me gay or making fun of my appearance, he became the bully. My one ally, my friend, was now the bully at home. The bullies didn't stop at deflating my self-esteem—they had stepped into my relationship with my father and messed with that too. They continued to hurt me and call me horrible things. What finally stopped them was punching two of them in the face when they called me a "fat pig" in class. I got nine days of suspension for that. The two other boys got only three days of suspension, which included the weekend. They were sent home on a Thursday afternoon with a three-day weekend. Without any way to prove what they'd been doing to me, I was just some kid making things up to get out of suspension. I was treated like some "at risk" juvenile who only knew violence. I hated fighting, and I didn't like hurting anyone, but I could only be pushed so far before I snapped. When Vivek asked me why I was ashamed, I couldn't help but think about this event in my life. I had stood up for myself, had done the right thing, yet I was left feeling worse about myself than when I lay on the ground in that field. I was ashamed to feel angry. I was ashamed that I wanted to fight. The kid getting hit with tennis ball–filled socks was no different than the kid in my dream. I was ashamed that I was scared.

In the morning, I woke up with an attitude, angry for how those questions made me feel. I was ready for Vivek and his stupid, mysterious questions. I was awake before everyone else and practiced my responses in my head. Argument after argument was rehearsed with tenacity. I was not going to look dumb again. It was as if I were planning a strategic battle, thinking through all my moves and countermoves, before Vivek had the chance to prepare. I was going to catch him off guard. I was ready to fight. Only one of us was going to walk away feeling stupid, and I was confident it would not be me.

When Vivek woke up, I just had this grin on my face, knowing something he didn't. He saw me looking at him and just laughed to himself, almost like he knew I had been planning my assault.

He came over and patted me on the back. He looked at me and said, "You know I am here to help, right? I don't intend to make you mad or to make you feel stupid, Ezra. I am here to challenge you. Last night those were easy questions. I told you when I met you this trip wouldn't be what you expected."

I tried to hold on to my anger, not wanting to give up the fight before it even began, but there was something calming about the way Vivek spoke to me. It was strange, almost like how I had felt looking at the sky the night before. There was so much chaos inside me, so much rage and anger over a simple question. When Vivek came over and talked to me, it felt like he was able to give order to all the chaos. A calmness. I didn't feel like he was a teacher scolding me for being an angry boy; I felt like he was a man calling me out. Like he was standing toe to toe with me, ready to show me who I was. Of course I couldn't allow him to know any of that. I had to stick to the battle plan. I gave him the fabricated attitude I woke up with, the attitude I had prepared for him while he slept.

After spending some time reigniting the morning fire, Vivek woke Daniel and Jordan up, and we all made breakfast.

"Eat up," Vivek told us. "You are going to need your energy. We are going on a hike."

The only hiking I had ever done was to this place called Mountain's Edge, which was basically a big hill that was less than half a mile. It was a joke, but it was convenient and safe. Knowing that I was about to do some real hiking scared me. I might not have looked like a chubby kid anymore, but that didn't mean I was in shape. I kept my facade in place, though, and we all piled into the van. The smell of teenage body odor and campfire smoke made for an uncomfortable car ride.

Vivek drove for quite some time. When he finally reached the end of the dirt road that we were on, he got a very excited look on his face and then proceeded to quickly accelerate into the desert. Clearly he had done this before, because he knew exactly where he was going. But to the three of us sitting in the back seat, this was uncharted territory, a mysterious no-man's-land. As my excitement grew, so did my fear. I was overwhelmed with these parallel realties that seemed to have taken ownership over me. I was excited to be traveling into the unknown, yet I was also terrified. I felt like an explorer searching an unknown land and knowing that, at any minute, we could be lost. It felt vaguely like my nightmare—intrigued by the idea of war, yet constantly searching for somewhere to hide, somewhere convenient and safe. As always, it was easy to hide my feelings from everyone, though from the looks on Daniel's and Jordan's faces, they felt the same. As we all sat paralyzed in our seats, expecting the vehicle to flip every time we hit another bump, we could see Vivek grinning from ear to ear. There was no fear in his eyes, just childlike enjoyment of four-wheeling through the desert.

Chapter 5
Remember to Trust

Vivek parked in front of a mysterious sandstone rock. From a distance, the rock hadn't seemed very big. It almost looked like the hill at Mountain's Edge. But up close, it seemed nothing short of Mount Everest.

Staring at the vast sandstone before me, I saw what looked like colorful ants moving up the rock. Curious, I took a second to look more closely. They weren't ants moving up the rock—they were rock climbers voyaging through a sea of stone. Using the climbers as a form of measurement, our understanding of this rock went from huge to gigantic.

Vivek stared at the rock and let out a deep sigh. It was clear he had a great appreciation for the beauty of this stone mountain. He turned to us with the same look of excitement we had seen in the van. "Get to climbing, boys!"

"Well, Vivek," exclaimed Daniel, "we would love nothing more than to do that, but how? None of us knows how to climb, and you didn't bring equipment."

Vivek grinned and simply said, "You will find a way. Of that I have no doubt." Once again, his smug, mysterious remarks drove us crazy.

We were clueless as to how to get up this rock. Every time we thought we saw a passage up, we would quickly discover it was too steep. We tried everything we could think of, including standing on one another's shoulders.

Daniel, being the athletic one in the group, got so frustrated at one point that he just picked a spot and started climbing only to make it up about five feet before falling on his butt. While Vivek was busy making sure Daniel wasn't hurt, Jordan and I ran around the area, trying to find the answer to our puzzle. We quickly came to the same conclusion that Daniel had: there was no way up on the surface without equipment. So Jordan and I switched gears and thought maybe the answer wasn't up. Maybe the answer was in. We searched high and low to find some kind of crack or slot canyon that might lead to the top, but still, we found nothing.

Just as we were about to give up, we spotted a group of people walking away from the rock. We ran over to them and asked how they had gotten to the top. They pointed to an area at the base of the mountain covered by a thicket of bushes, but before they could give us directions, we saw them making eye contact with Vivek. He was shaking his head: *Don't tell them.* They laughed and said, "Sorry, boys," and then walked away. We were failing this test too.

Jordan and I finally sat down, exhausted and frustrated. "Stupid freaking hiking trip," I said, hoping Vivek could hear me. I picked up a rock and threw it as hard as I could at the bushes at the base of this Mount Everest–sized stone—the same ones the group had pointed at. To my surprise, the rock continued through the bushes. I never heard it stop. I got up and looked at the bushes and kicked them a few times. I wasn't exactly sure what the kicking was meant to accomplish. Maybe I thought Frodo or some other hobbit was playing games with me. After I learned that nothing was in the bushes, I looked inside and found a hole in the side of the rock, big enough for even Vivek, the largest of us, to make it through. Suddenly my exhaustion turned into excitement, and I quickly called everyone over and started to crawl through the hole. I felt like Indiana Jones finding the lost ark. Daniel was the next one through, then Jordan and Vivek.

I looked at Vivek with so much excitement, awaiting his praise.

"Good work, Ezra," he said. "You found a way in but not a way up. This doesn't get us up the rock. Don't get too excited."

I didn't care that there was more to the riddle; it was clear I was the winner.

The hole led to a slot canyon big enough for only one person at a time, so the four of us created a single-file line. Vivek thought it was only fitting to let me lead the group since I had found the hole. We walked for what felt like miles and miles with no luck finding a way up the mountain. Yet we all sensed that Vivek knew exactly where we were going. We probed him with questions, trying to figure out if he knew where we were heading or even if we were heading in the right direction, which seemed like a stupid question because we could only go forward or backward. As usual, he just smiled and said something mysterious and annoying like, "I guess we will find out."

All of my excitement about finding the entrance soon vanished, making me wish I'd never said anything about it. Poor Daniel seemed ready to pass out, which wasn't too surprising considering how much climbing he'd done trying to find the entrance. The farther and farther we went, the more Daniel's eyes welled up with tears; he had given up on the adventure long before we even found the entrance. I couldn't blame him either; he really didn't want to be on this trip at all. Daniel was a little older than Jordan and me. He was seventeen, and Jordan and I were fourteen. Two days before the trip, Daniel's girlfriend called him and said that there was a lot on her mind and that they needed to talk. Daniel didn't hesitate; he started walking to her house since she lived only two blocks away from him. On his way to see her, Daniel got a text from her saying, "You aren't the man I thought you were," and that they couldn't be together anymore. She didn't even have the guts to wait to say it to him in person. She just laid it all out over a text.

Daniel said he didn't care, that he played it cool and that he could have any girl he wanted, but we all knew he was just holding back the tears. Every couple of hours, I could see him rereading the texts even though we had no reception in the cave. I guess he was hoping that he'd missed some sign of hope. At one point I looked over his shoulder and could see his blue bubbles on the screen were like novels and hers were barely a sentence long. Daniel was the guy everyone looked up to, the guy every girl wanted to be with. He was smart, athletic, and creative. I mean, Daniel was the guy both Jordan and I looked up to.

Daniel's mom was a floor nurse at a hospital. She worked nights to support the two of them. Even though his mom was home during the day, she was usually sleeping to get ready for her next twelve-hour shift, and her days off were spent catching up on sleep. Daniel didn't really have a parent to talk to about the breakup. This had been a tough week for him, and hiking through Dante's *Inferno* didn't really seem to be helping. It was humbling to see him on the verge of crying over this riddle Vivek had set up for us. Here was the guy we saw as the picture of the ideal man. To us, Daniel had it all together, but it was clear today that he was just as screwed up as the rest of us. He was scared and ashamed of something ... just like me.

After a while, none of us liked this hike very much. The excitement had worn off, and we were all tired. Daniel, taking the lead in our protest, decided to sit down and just quit. He looked at Vivek and exclaimed, "You are a jerk, man. You drag us out into the middle of nowhere saying you want us to 'find our name' but don't do anything to help us. You suck, man! You can keep walking, but I am sitting here and waiting for you to come back."

Vivek bent down on one knee and looked at Daniel. "What is your name?"

"Man, get a freaking clue. I don't want to play your dumb game. My name is Daniel. That's all I need to know." Daniel swiped the ground with his foot, kicking up dirt.

"Okay, Daniel, what does your name mean?"

"Man, I already told you. I don't care. Leave me the hell alone, okay? That's what my name means. Got it?"

Vivek sat down next to Daniel. He didn't seem fazed by Daniel's anger. His body language and calm voice suggested he was very skilled at handling these kinds of reactions. "Daniel was a Hebrew prophet whose story is told in the book of Daniel in the Torah. It has very deep roots in Jewish history. All of your names do, actually. Now, I don't mean to focus on religion—this trip isn't about that—but most of our names have deep roots in religion, and no matter what we believe, we can learn something from anyone. Our names have power, and those who have been called Daniel before you were strong characters in history. Daniel lived during the Jewish captivity in Babylon, where he served in the court of the king. This means he lived in a time when his country was taken over by another and he served the king—his captor. Daniel became very popular with that king, rising to prominence by interpreting the king's dreams. *Daniel* means 'God is my judge.' Though he was a slave to the king who stole his country and killed his people, he still commanded strength and never settled on what he believed."

Daniel started to relax a little. His shoulders showed a slow progression downward, indicating that something Vivek was saying was helping.

Vivek continued, "In the Jewish history, Daniel did some amazing things, even spent a night in a cage with lions. He was fearless." Vivek began to raise his voice to emphasize the power of this story. "And do you know why? Not because he knew anything that you and I didn't—it was because he trusted that he didn't need to have all the answers. Do you know where you are going, Daniel?"

Still looking down at the ground, Daniel shrugged. "I have no idea, man."

Vivek matched Daniel's soft tone and said, "What if I told you that around this corner there is a ladder that will lead us straight to the top of this rock? What if I told you that up there is a lunch already made for you in this backpack of mine, Daniel? And what if I told you that all you need to get out of this small canyon is to trust? Trust that I have your best interests in mind. Trust that I am not playing games with you guys."

Lifting his head up and looking sorrowfully into Vivek's eyes, Daniel said, "I don't know you, and I want to trust you. You are right that I am clueless right now. I have no idea where we are going. Out of the four of us, you are the only one who has a smile on your face. So I may not trust you yet, but I trust you know something I don't. This lunch you packed better be good."

Vivek stood and offered a hand to Daniel. The four of us, now ready to press on, dusted ourselves off and moved forward.

Vivek decided it would probably be best if he led the group the rest of the way. We did not have to walk far to get past the bend, and sure enough, there was a ladder anchored to the canyon wall and hanging from an opening above us. Daniel was the first to go up. The way he ran up the ladder, it was as if he was fighting for his life, climbing his way to freedom. Jordan was next.

While Jordan was making his ascent, Vivek put his hand on my shoulder and said, "Do you get it yet?"

"Do I get what?" I responded, confusion in my voice.

"Why we are here, why we are doing all of this."

"No, I don't, man, and if I am being honest, you are starting to seem a little crazy," I said, chuckling awkwardly, as if hiding the truth of my statement.

Vivek let out a loud laugh, seeming to enjoy this idea that he was crazy. "You know what, Ezra? You are right; I am a little crazy, but name one man who isn't. You are a good kid, Ezra. You remind me of why it is that I do all of this, why I reopen these wounds in my heart every time I do this trip." Vivek paused to grab the railing of the ladder. "It is to challenge brilliant young men like yourself."

Then he started walking up the steps, leaving me profoundly confused again.

What wounds is he talking about? I wondered.

What does he mean I remind him of why he is doing this?

I eagerly called out to Vivek, hoping for some insight before he made his way to the top. "Hey, Vivek, what are you talking about, man? What wounds do you open? You look fine to me."

He just smiled his usual smug smile and said, "I guess you will find out, Ezra." Then he kept climbing.

I sat there at the bottom of the ladder, alone with my thoughts. My mind filled with uneasy chaos. What is this trip? What is even going on? I kept asking myself. Above all else, I kept hearing the question, *Why do you fight, Ezra?* This question haunted me. Though I knew I was only shouting distance from everyone, I felt completely alone. And though I knew exactly where the ladder went, I felt lost. I was lost. I sat there, feeling helpless, tears collecting in my eyes. What do I do? I asked myself. Almost immediately, I heard, "Remember to trust, Ezra." I looked up and saw Vivek's head popping out over the top of the hole. For a second, I thought God was saying hello.

Chapter 6
What Do You Know of the Civil War?

I began to ascend the ladder after I finished pondering the words Vivek left me with. More and more light filled the canyon with every step I took. As I got closer and closer to the top, I could feel the heaviness of my burdens lift off me, as if I were leaving them behind in the shadow-filled canyon. They weren't gone by any means—I still had a lot of questions that I didn't have answers to—but as I made my way to the top, my perspective changed. My literal, view was no longer dark, damp, and tiny, but it was full of light, beautiful, and open. In a much more profound sense, though, my mind's view was the same. It was no longer dark, damp, and tiny but shared the same openness and light that I now stood enjoying. Leaving my burdens in the canyon below, my view changed in every sense of the word as I began to raise.

When I made it to the top, I could see for miles and miles. Our campsite from last night was far in the distance. Everything looked like it was either dirt or rocks, yet the beauty was captivating. I was in awe of everything I saw. I put my hand to my chest and felt my escalated heartbeat pounding against my hand. It was the same sound of war drums, echoing the identity of the vast desert before me.

"Hey, loner, want to come join us, or are you too busy being a girl?" Jordan asked while holding his belly, trying to contain his laughter. Jordan always thought his jokes were hilarious, but they always had the same punch line: "Too busy being a girl?" Everyone around him was always confused, but he would just snort with laughter in response to his own joke. As I got to know Jordan, though, his jokes became funny because he was in fact the only one who couldn't see they showed his age all too well.

I walked over to the group. They had already started passing out the lunch that Vivek had made for us. Each sandwich was different and had our names written on the plastic. Daniel had a sub that looked like it contained only meat and cheese, the typical "man's sandwich." Jordan had a boring ham sandwich with extra mayo. Mine was a bagel with cream cheese and salami. No doubt our sandwich differences were yet another symbol by Vivek that we all had a "unique identity" as men, but all of us were too hungry to comment or, to be honest, to care.

Jordan handed me my bagel, saying, "Here is your

bagel, princess. Would you like Prince Charming with that?"

We all laughed because that didn't even make sense, but that was Jordan with his nonsensical humor. This unlikely group of gentlemen sat together as champions, as if we had just climbed Mount Everest. The tears, confusion, and anger now seemed like a distant memory. All that was left was a great sense of accomplishment.

Vivek gave me a knowing smile. "I think Ezra has something to say."

"I do?" I asked, wondering how he knew what I was thinking.

Vivek let out one of his signature chuckles. "I think you know what I am talking about, Ezra."

Hoping we were on the same page, I responded, "Just wanted to say good job, fellas. We did it. We made it to the top."

Everyone gave a nod and a big smile to acknowledge what we had accomplished and continued eating our food. There was no need for some big celebration. A nod and a smile spoke more to the shared experience than celebration could. We had all struggled with our journey to the top, and we had all left our fears and sorrows in the canyon below and sat upon the mountain as victors. Each one of us felt a sense of pride within that needed not to be celebrated but held onto, enjoyed. We were champions—no one could convince us otherwise.

We sat at the top of that rock for quite some time, just laughing, having fun, and telling stories. Jordan let out a few farts, and we would all bust out laughing. There's something so comical, at least to the teenage boy, about a fart, no matter what kind of day you have had. We had quickly forgotten the struggles of getting to this peak; we were living in the present moment. We sat up there, looking far out into the desert and seeing the world pass by as the sun slowly dipped below the rocks in the distance. The warm breeze filled our lungs, and the sand gently grazed our cheeks, caressing our faces as if to remind us to hold on to this moment. I sat there silently as everyone continued to talk, staring off and soaking up as much detail as I could, trying to take a mental photograph of what was before me. I was overcome with the same feeling of peace I had that previous night. As I looked around the valley, I could see animals running and birds flying throughout the area. I could smell the fresh air that I was not accustomed to in the city. I couldn't see the city or any buildings. We were all wild and free. If you had asked me in that moment what I was feeling, I would have told you I felt home. Something about that place, about nature, made my heart feel whole. I was in love with it all.

We all shared a moment of silence as we stared off into the distance and watched the sun slowly go down. Meanwhile, Vivek began to make a fire.

Toward the end of sunset, things turned from childish fun, laughing at farts and Jordan's stupid jokes, to a more serious mood.

"It is time for a story," Vivek said ominously.

We all sensed panic in his voice, as if he had no

desire to enter this part of the camping trip, this portion of the night. We could see in his eyes that he was nervous and anxious to tell this story. Was this what he had been talking about before? I couldn't help but think that this was the wound he had been referring to. His cold demeanor made it clear that this was why we had come on this hike, maybe even the focal point of the camping trip. We all gathered in a circle around Vivek as he built up the courage to speak. Staring at the fire, Vivek took a few deep sighs and appeared to be rehearsing his lines in his head. Finally he spoke.

"What do you know about the Civil War?" Vivek asked.

Jordan raised his hand. "It was the war between the North and South to free the slaves."

"Do you all agree?" asked Vivek, and we all nodded. "What if I told you that the Civil War had more depth to it? That there was more at stake than just freeing the slaves?"

We all seemed puzzled.

"The Civil War was a fight between right and wrong. It was a fight between good and evil. The North thought that they were right and that their cause was good. The South thought that they were right and that their cause was good. What if I told you that the Civil War was a fight for the name of this country? In fact, it is the same fight that brought me and you to the top of this rock. It is the same fight in every person, their fight for their identity. America, as a whole, was asking the infamous question, Who am I? Answering that question led to fighting for what was right, fighting for equal rights for slaves."

I heard what Vivek was saying, but I was confused. Why would this be something that was so hard to talk about? It seemed like just another history lesson.

I asked Vivek, "Why are you telling us this?"

He gave us a stern look and responded quickly with a harsh tone. "Because you are fighting for your life, for your identity. To end the cycle of pain and suffering that those before have fallen into over and over again. You three are asking yourselves the same question, Who am I?"

Everyone became dead silent. It wasn't what he said that scared us; it was his tone that scared us most of all. With a stern but sad look on his face, Vivek looked back down at the fire and said, "I wish someone would have taken me to a rock like this when I was young. I wish I had learned what I want to share with you before it was too late, before I lost my ..."

"Your what, Vivek?" Daniel asked.

"Nothing, son, never mind. I need all of you to just listen and think, that's all I am asking of you."

"Think about what, man? What is going on?" Daniel asked, sounding slightly panicked.

"Daniel, you remember how I asked you to trust that I know what I am doing? Trust me." Though we were all desperate for answers, we had none. All we could do was trust as Vivek began to tell us a story.

Chapter 7
Saul Treeborn

On July 21, 1841, a child was born named Saul
Treeborn. Saul was born in New York City, which was
and still is one of the most progressive cities in the
United States. Saul was born into a wealthy family. His
dad was an investor, mostly in steel companies and
freighters that brought goods from other nations. His
father was a very smart man and knew where to put his
money, and by the time Saul was five, his father had
made a name for himself, but not without a cost. Saul's
father was rarely ever home; in fact, he wouldn't be there
for months at a time because he was tending to his
business. Saul's mother raised him, and his father made
the money—a lot of money. There was no worry about
money in the Treeborn family. Despite Saul's absent
father, Saul had a very easy childhood, seeing that there
was nothing his father's money couldn't fix.

Saul's father sent him to a prestigious boarding
school downtown, and by the age of eight, Saul knew

three languages: French, Spanish, and of course, English. Saul had an extremely bright future as long as he had his mother's love and his father's money. But even with everything that Saul had, there was still something missing. Something that would plague him for his whole life.

Despite all of his advantages in life and all the great things that were handed to him, Saul was angry and bitter. Was he mad that his father wasn't around? Was he bitter that a woman was raising him? Saul struggled with this anger, this fire in his heart, every waking day of his life, yet if you looked at him, he seemed like he had it all together. He was the picture of success at a young age.

Every year that passed, Saul felt his heart die a little at a time. He kept getting into fights at school and getting into trouble during class. Saul began to turn to women to stop this pain, and women sure did love him. He was a natural ladies' man. He was strong, handsome, and rich. He even was the captain of the football team. It was rumored that he took three separate girls to a dance at his school, and they all knew but didn't care. Everything seemed great, and for a long time, the women stopped the pain he felt. Every time he was with another woman, he felt like a man, like that cold, dark heart of his became warm for just a second. But it was only a second. That moment would fade quickly, and he would leave each woman as broken as he was. A few years went on like this for Saul until, one day, it all came crashing down.

On March 14, 1857, Saul was in his dorm room when the police came and asked to speak with him. They took him aside and told him that his father had been shot and killed the night before. Apparently, his father's investments were going south, and he had borrowed money from the wrong people to cover his losses.

Saul fell to his knees and wept. He wasn't sad that his father had died—he didn't care what happened to his father, because his father didn't care about him. He was sad that he never got the chance to tell his father how much he hated his guts. The only thing he had of his father's was a pistol with an ivory handle that was left to him in his father's will. Everything else was sold to pay off his debts. Saul swore that he would never be like his father. He swore that he would love his future wife and be there for his children. The hatred for his father became stronger and stronger.

Five months later, Saul met a woman named Emma Grace and fell head over heels for her. After a few months of dating, Saul asked Emma to marry him, and on February 4, 1858, they said, "I do." They loved each other desperately. Saul would wake up every morning in awe that such a great, wonderful woman would love someone like him. He would find her flowers every time her vase was empty. There was nothing that Saul would not do for Emma and nothing Emma would not do for Saul.

Saul was content in the world, and for the first time that he could remember, that anger inside of him was maintained, as if it were locked away in a cage. He knew it was there, much like you know the lions in a zoo are there and still dangerous. But you also know that from the outside the cage, you are safe. Saul was happy, even joyful, and deeply in love, but that wasn't enough to stop the cycle of anger within him.

About five years into the marriage, Saul found it more and more difficult to keep his anger and temper caged. He was constantly yelling at Emma and making her feel like it was all her fault that their marriage was crumbling. Saul was still very much in love with Emma, that had not changed, but it wasn't enough to keep his anger at bay anymore. Saul had started to realize that he was nothing without his wife and job. Saul was only seventeen when he married Emma; he didn't know who he was as a man. At twenty-two, he felt that his entire identity was wrapped up in being either Emma's husband or a successful businessman. There was nothing unique, nothing personable, about Saul's name or identity. Just an empty shell of a man going about pretending as he walked through his daily routine: work then home ... work then home ... work then home.

One night after work, Saul and Emma got into a very heated argument over some petty thing. Saul left the house, feeling lost and alone. He was angry and depressed. Feeling like a kid again, he couldn't help but think of his father, and as his mind shifted toward his father, so did the blame. He found his mind racing with arguments, things he wished he could have confronted his father about. With so much anger and so many anxious thoughts running through his head, Saul found himself unable to focus. So, he thought it would be a good idea to get drunk, hoping he would forget all the pain. His secretary, Jill, who had always liked Saul, happened to be at the same bar that he was at that night, and she came over to have a drink with him.

After a few drinks with Jill, Saul started to feel more and more attracted to her, and he felt like he was almost watching himself making a decision that he knew he would regret. It wasn't long before Saul reverted to his old ways of coping with his anger. He and Jill both decided to go back to Jill's place, and they began to have an affair.

Saul went home to Emma afterward. At that point, it was probably eleven or twelve at night. Emma could smell the alcohol on his breath and a woman's perfume on his clothes, but knowing he left because they were fighting, she figured he just went to a bar. Emma trusted Saul and gave him the benefit of the doubt.

The next morning, Saul woke up feeling overwhelmed with grief and hating himself for what he had done, but he did not know what to do. He knew that he had made a huge mistake and found the anger and guilt from his childhood building up in him again. He loved his wife. He had no idea why he would have an affair with someone when his heart belonged to Emma, but it was becoming clear he didn't quite know anything about himself truthfully. He went downstairs to where his wife was making breakfast, and he kissed her good morning.

Though she felt his anguish, Emma did not skip a beat that morning; she acted as if Saul was a saint and made him a good breakfast. As Saul walked to work, his head was full of thoughts about what he should do. He knew that Jill would remember everything and that she would not let things end with a one-night stand. He thought of ways to fire her or get her to leave the company, but he knew that was wrong. He tried to have arguments with Jill in his head, blaming her for the mistake that he had made the night before. Thought after thought was filled with regret and anger. What should I do, God? Saul prayed over and over again. He was not a religious man but found prayer was needed to forgive himself for this.

When he got to the office, the first person to greet him at the door was Jill. She sure did look beautiful. She had her hair down. Her makeup was just perfect, and she had the same perfume on from the night before, making his heart race. Saul called Jill into his office to explain the situation to her and to tell her that it couldn't happen again. Before he knew it, he was kissing her once again and making the same mistake that was causing him so much pain. This went on and on for quite some time, and every late night at work was filled with bad decisions and lustful shame.

Every time that Saul came home, his wife would smell the perfume on his clothes and the liquor on his breath and know something was going on, but she would lie to herself. She would tell herself that it was in her head or that she was imagining everything. She quickly became depressed and even more distant from Saul, and he knew why but couldn't bring himself to tell her what was going on. He still loved Emma, but he couldn't seem to satisfy the craving he had inside of him. He was still looking to fill that void in his life, to extinguish that fire that was burning inside of him. And if he was being honest with himself, it was exciting. He was no longer just a husband and businessman going from work to home ... work to home. Life had secrets now. Though they were painful and stressful secrets. His identity was taking shape, a shape Saul was not proud of, but it was a shape that was more dynamic than before, and that was something that excited him.

The only thing that kept Emma from losing it altogether was the fact that they were trying to have a child. That was Emma's hope and the only thing she wanted. Every day she became more and more depressed from the lies of her husband but also the lies she was telling herself. Saul knew that he needed to do something but didn't know what. Saul went to the local Catholic Church and asked the priest what he needed to do, and the priest simply said, "Confess." So, Saul started spilling his life to the priest, but the priest just started laughing. He looked at Saul and said, "I am not the person you need to confess to—it is your wife." Saul's heart just dropped. The thought of telling Emma made him run out of the church and vomit on the sidewalk. He was so scared, but he knew the priest was right. He went back inside and prayed with the priest for strength. Then he went to the nearest flower stand and bought

Emma the biggest bundle he could find. At that point, he was feeling confident, so he ran home. When he opened the door, he saw Emma—sitting in a chair, crying. As Saul pushed the door open a little farther, he saw Jill sitting there talking with Emma, crying as well.

It turned out that Jill could not live with the shame and guilt of sleeping with a married man anymore and had told Emma. Saul's life went crashing down in that single moment. Saul dropped to his knees, and the flowers fell to the ground. Jill got up and kissed his cheek before she walked out.

Saul turned pale and cold, and his hands became like ice. He was in shock of everything that had just happened. He looked down at his bluish hands and watched as his tears slid off them. He only did this for a few seconds, but to him, it felt like an eternity.

Finally, taking in the reality of everything, Saul crawled over to Emma, weeping and trying to explain to her that he was going to tell her and that was what the flowers were for. He could not get one word out without tears covering his lips. He knew at this point that he had lost Emma forever.

Emma took a break from her sobbing, looked at Saul, and said, "I love you so much." Then she got up and kissed his lips before she walked out of the room.

Saul fell over on his butt with bewilderment. Did she just forgive me? he found himself asking. He couldn't comprehend what she meant by her words and her kiss, but he didn't care. At that point, Saul saw hope for his relationship with Emma. He thought of all the steps he was going to take to make things right from this point on. He was in so much shock that Emma was so forgiving of him and the shameful things that he had done but was not going to question her loyalty. Saul found joy again. He jumped to his feet and began to dance. He quickly turned his face to Heaven and praised God for answering his prayers, but a loud noise interrupted him ... *BANG!* ... and then a thump. Saul ran upstairs to see what had happened.

When he got upstairs, he saw his father's ivory-handled pistol lying on the floor. He took another step forward, and he saw Emma's feet sticking out from the doorframe. Saul took another step forward, and he saw his beautiful Emma lying there lifeless.

His wife had taken her own life with the pistol that his father left him in his will.

Chapter 8
Bull Run

We all sat there in shock, not quite understanding why Vivek was telling us this story. It seemed a little too heavy, a little too dark, for a group of teenagers. Vivek wept as he told us about Emma's death, almost as if Emma was someone he loved very much, yet there was no way he would have known her—the story was from the 1800s. We waited for Vivek to talk, but he kept weeping.

I looked over at Jordan and saw that he was crying too. We all knew why. His parents were considering divorce right now, and they were going through couples' counseling. Jordan's mom had had an affair, just like Saul, with her high school boyfriend. Jordan said his mother promised it was a one-time thing and his dad had been very forgiving, but it was clear the affair was eating away at everyone in the family. The story Vivek told probably scared Jordan. Daniel scooted closer to him and put his arm around his shoulder.

Jordan looked up, wiping the tears from his eyes. "Vivek, I thought that the pistol didn't exist yet. Like, I thought that pistols back then were only the ones you loaded with, like, gunpowder and a ball. How did she do that so quickly?"

I knew it wasn't the right time, but I almost burst out laughing. Jordan had gone from crying to asking a silly question like that. Vivek gave me a very stern look and then looked at Jordan for a second, like he was not sure what to say.

Vivek wiped the tears from his eyes and said, "You'll understand soon, Jordan. Just hang tight."

Jordan, Daniel, and I looked at one another, not sure what Vivek meant. To us, the story seemed over. Apparently, there was more to tell, and Vivek seemed to dread the next half of the story more than he did the first half.

"Before I continue, does anyone have any more questions?" Vivek asked.

"Don't you think suicide, death, and all this is a little much for kids our age?" I asked.

Vivek shook his head. "I don't think so, Ezra. Our society hides our youth from death and heavy topics like this, but when we are trying to understand who we are, we can't hide from such things. Death can be a beautiful reminder that we need to focus on the important matters in life, to let go of the pain and bitterness of yesterday and focus on a better tomorrow. Buddhists start every morning with a practice called the Five Remembrances, where they recite phrases that remind them that one day, they will die. It's the idea of impermanence, that nothing is permanent and everything has an end. They do this to remind themselves to live, to enjoy the present moment. It isn't just adults who do this; children do it too. I can't help any of you find your name, help you find your identity, if I can't first help you understand how precious life is. That only happens in light of death." He looked up at the stars. "Some of these stars are already dead; the light just hasn't reached us yet. No one looks at a child and says the stars aren't beautiful, that they aren't old enough to enjoy them. In the right context, in the context of what I am trying to accomplish, impermanence can be beautiful. Now, are you guys ready to keep going with the story?"

We all nodded. Vivek took a deep breath and continued.

Saul was a mess after Emma killed herself. When they found Saul, he was holding Emma's body, kissing her forehead and saying to himself over and over, "I'm so sorry, Em. I am so sorry." Emma's funeral was the following weekend, and Saul couldn't bring himself to come near his family or Emma's. He watched from behind a tree. He started drinking every night, and many nights landed him in the hospital. A month or so went by, and he tried to find Jill, hoping to relieve some of his pain, but Jill just pushed him away. The thrill of the affair was gone, and what had made Saul the man Jill liked was also gone. The only thing that Saul knew how to do anymore was drink, and he did that well.

On April 12, 1861, war broke out between the North and the South. Saul, living in New York City, was being recruited by the Union Army to join the fight, but he would not do it. Saul just found himself at the bar every night, trying to kill himself slowly, the cowardly way. He tried his hardest to end his life but just couldn't do it for fear of never seeing Emma again. One night Saul got into a fight with someone at the bar. He lay on the ground while two men kicked his face in. When the men were finished with him, they threw him in a dark alley. After a few hours of lying on the cold, hard ground, covered in blood, praying he was finally about to die, a police officer found him and got him some help.

They cleaned Saul up at the hospital, and the officer took Saul's statement about what had happened. When Saul told the officer his name, the officer realized who he was. He looked at Saul's bruised face and just shook his head. "Saul Treeborn. Your father would be disappointed in you. I knew your father when he was a police officer before you were born. Before he made enough money to forget about everyone who cared about him. We were partners. Great man, your father, but look at you."

Saul got out of the bed, limped over to the officer, and spit in his face. The officer tackled Saul and used the bed restraints to keep him there.

"What the hell is wrong with you, Saul? Are you stupid?" the officer asked.

Saul responded, "You don't know a damn thing

about my father. He was not a great man. He was a waste of life. You can go to hell and spend as much time with that horrible excuse of a father as you want."

The officer wiped the spit off his face and grinned. "You know what, Saul? You are probably right. I never took the time to get to know your father outside of work. I should have, and I am sorry for that. The bartender at the pub you were at tonight is pressing charges, and unless you have any information you ain't telling me, I am going to have to take you to jail. I have an alternative for you though: join the military to fight those guys down south, and I will say that you escaped. I owe that to your father."

Saul sat there thinking long and hard and finally accepted the proposal.

Over the course of the next few months, Saul sobered up and tried to come to grips with what had happened to Emma. He found himself going to bed almost every night, crying as he thought about how much he missed her. Oh, how he would love to just tell her one last time that he was sorry for what he had done. He wanted to tell her that he loved her and that he would do anything to kiss her again. Saul hated what he had done to her but knew he couldn't change it.

In the military, Saul found some semblance of peace and did his best to work through the pains of his loss and deal with the anger he had for his father. Yet every day he prayed for forgiveness and that God would take his life so that he could see Emma again. Saul knew that he wasn't through on this earth yet though. Who am

I? Saul still found himself asking.

July 21, 1861, the first major battle of the Civil War. It was the Battle of Bull Run. Saul found himself on the front lines in Virginia near the city of Manassas, ready to fight for the North. Saul was terrified as the Confederate Army marched forward. He could hear the sounds of their feet stomping on the ground and their heavy breathing. It sounded like a beast moving closer and closer to devour them. Saul wished that he could be in the arms of Emma—to have something to fight for. He looked around and could only see men hungry for a fight. How can I fight all of these men? he asked himself. He planted his feet firmly on the ground and looked his enemy in the face. Ready to fight but terrified, Saul counted down as his enemy ran toward him. Five. Saul took a deep breath. Four. He checked his weapon. Three. He aimed his gun at his enemy. Two. He fired his weapon. One. He drew his sword. Time for battle.

Under the rifle fire of Saul and his men, the enemy's front lines dropped, and those after them charged at the armies of the North. Saul went hand to hand with the enemy. It was chaos everywhere. Screaming and cries of war surrounded him. He saw his fellow troops dead on the ground. So much chaos and anger, and yet for some reason ... Saul could make sense of it all. It was ugly and brutal, but the chaos made sense to him.

At the end of the battle, Saul was commanded to walk through the field and see if any of his comrades were alive. He searched for survivors, but few had made it. Saul looked out at the sea of bodies. So much death and chaos, yet he knew there was hope somewhere on this battlefield. He stopped and looked for any movement that might signal a survivor, and sure enough, he saw something off in the distance. He moved toward what he had seen, checking the bodies along the way. When he got closer, he discovered that the movement was coming from an enemy soldier. He moved slowly toward his enemy and drew his sword. When he got close, the solider stabbed Saul in the right shoulder and ran away. Saul chased after the soldier despite the extreme pain in his shoulder. Saul knew he was in great danger—no one knew where he was, but it didn't matter. He needed to catch this guy.

Saul ran as fast as he could to catch up with this solider, but it seemed like every step he took, his enemy was three steps ahead. The soldier's stride imitated that of a bull determined to make its escape. Saul found himself screaming for backup, but to his knowledge, no one could hear him. This bull just kept on running and running as Saul started to lose his strength. Suddenly, as luck would have it, the solider tripped over a rock and fell to the ground. Lying facedown in the grass, the enemy soldier moaned in pain. Saul approached slowly and kicked aside all of the man's weapons. Then he turned the man over using his foot, while his bayonet was drawn, so he could see the man's face.

When Saul finally saw the man's face, he could not believe his own eyes. Tears pooled in his eyes as he slowly dropped to his knees. Filled with confusion and anger, he began punching the soldier's chest uncontrollably. Some of Saul's comrades came running over. They pried Saul off him and took the other solider as a prisoner.

"Saul, what the hell are you doing, man? What is wrong? Why are you crying?" they asked. His fellow men were trying to understand the hatred they were seeing in Saul.

Saul, wiping the tears from his eyes and smearing the blood from his knuckles on his face in the process, looked at his friends and simply said:

"That solider is my father."

Chapter 9
A Scared Heart

"Wait, wait, wait, Vivek. His dad is alive?" Daniel asked.

Jordan jumped in: "You said Saul's father was killed because of some bad business deal or because he pissed off the mob or something."

"I know this seems crazy and you weren't expecting a plot twist, but I promise, if you guys bear with me, I will explain everything," Vivek said.

What started as a boring story about some guy from the 1800s now had our complete and undivided attention. We sat anxiously waiting to hear the story's conclusion.

"I know we have been out here for a while now, boys, and I promise you that I am almost done, and then we can go to bed. So, where was I?" Vivek asked.

"You were just blowing our minds," Daniel answered.

Vivek laughed. "Oh, that's right—he found his

father. How could I forget?" He continued with the story.

Saul was handcuffed and placed in secured barracks, under suspicion of being a traitor. Seeing that Saul's father was the enemy, Saul's captain wondered if Saul was working with him. Saul was confused, hurt, and afraid. All Saul could think was that he was going crazy with the grief he had for Emma and that the battle must be causing him to see things.

Is that really my father? Saul asked himself. No, no way. Your father is dead, Saul. Get it together. You are seeing things.

Saul knew he wasn't seeing things, but he was sure hoping he could talk himself into believing that. Why is my father still alive? he thought. And why is my father fighting for the South?

Saul felt like he'd been thrown in jail. He knew that he was going to be in the secured barracks for a while, stuck in this dark cage while he was investigated. His father, no doubt, was probably getting better treatment being a prisoner of war than some "spy" or "traitor" like himself. Saul sat in the dark, blaming his father for where he was and how he had gotten there. He thought about all the times his father wasn't there for him. Like when he broke up with his first girlfriend and needed to talk to someone other than his mother about it. He thought about how desperately he wanted his father when his friend had died from sickness in school and he

was so scared that he was going to die too. Or the time
that someone who had never met Saul's dad called his
father a fairy, suggesting he never existed in the first
place. Saul had punched that kid right in the mouth and
shut him up real quick. He'd felt so proud about
standing up for his father's honor, and when he got
home, there was no father around to tell about it. Saul
also thought about the moment he found out his father
had died, how he was so angry with his father for dying,
so mad that he'd left him and his mother without ever
saying good-bye. Without ever saying that he loved him
or that he was proud of him.

How could you just leave without saying good-bye,
Dad? Saul found himself thinking. You were never there
for me; you were never there for anyone. You cared
more about your goddamn money than you did about
me. I hate you. You selfish jerk, you can't even say good-
bye to your own son?

Saul found himself feeling like a little kid again,
angry and alone. All the hurt he had pushed down came
to the surface in the blink of an eye, and how did he
have to deal with it all? In a jail cell that his father had
landed him in. Saul had never felt so alone.

He spent the next several hours sobbing over the
anger he had for his father. Finally, when it seemed that
he could cry no more, he stood up and stuck his hands
through the bars. He saw his friend Ben off in the
distance. "Ben. Hey, Ben! Get over here, man."

Ben approached Saul, looking over his shoulder.
"What? I can't be talking to you. You are in a world of

trouble. Why did you tell the captain your dad was dead when he asked if you had any family in the South? You know you just made yourself look like a liar and a traitor?"

Saul replied, "I didn't even know he was alive, Ben, let alone fighting for the South. I am just as shocked as the captain."

"What do you want, Saul? Make it quick."

Saul whispered, "I need booze, man, anything you can get your hands on. I can't be in this cage with all these thoughts while I'm sober, man. Please help me."

Ben stood there thinking about how much trouble he could get in for giving Saul booze, but Saul had saved his life more than once. "Okay, man. Give me an hour, but only this once. After this, you owe me one if you get out of this mess," Ben said.

Saul lay back down on the cold, muddy ground and began to sob again. He had been sober and on the right track for a while, yet all he could think about now was getting drunk. He didn't want to be alone with his thoughts anymore. All the depression and guilt he had worked through about Emma came rushing back. Everything that he had been escaping came to him in an instant.

Saul covered himself with some hay and curled up in a ball, hoping to fall asleep. The oh-so-familiar feeling of wanting to die rushed over him. He closed his eyes and said a prayer: "Lord, you are no better than my father. In fact, you are just like him. I needed you in so many different ways throughout my life, and yet where were you? You were probably helping someone 'holier than thou.' You help those who have it all together, yet I have been hurting my whole life, and you have never helped me. What makes you any different than my real father? You abandoned me ... once again. So, I am going to make you this promise, God. I will leave you alone. You get me out of this mess you put me in, and I will never bother you anymore. I won't ask anything of you anymore if you just fix what you messed up. I don't want anything to do with a god that abandons me in my time of need anyway. You have been a waste of my time." Saul finished his prayer and fell asleep.

When Saul woke up a few hours later, there was a bottle of rum sitting at the front of his cage. He crawled over immediately, grabbed the bottle, and took the cork out. You would have sworn that Saul was a man dying of thirst the way he drank that bottle down. Saul saw it as his lifeline, his way out of all this pain and misery. He had hoped it would kill him, but at least it would just numb the pain. It didn't take Saul very long to finish the bottle, and when he did, he started talking to himself until he saw Emma. He knew that he was just drunk and she wasn't there, but he didn't care; he missed her so much.

"Emma? What are you doing ... how are you here?" he asked. "I have missed you so much. I am so sorry for what I did to you. I hate myself so much. I would do anything to get you back, Emma. Please don't go anywhere. Please be real. Sweetheart, please tell me this is real."

Tears ran down his face as he desperately tried to touch her, but no matter how close he got to her, she seemed to always be too far to touch.

"Emma, I love you. Please forgive me, sweetheart, please."

"Shh, Saul, it's okay," Emma said with her sweet, soft voice. "I forgive you, and I wasn't lying when I told you I love you. What happened was not your fault. It was my choice to leave, and I am so sorry, Saul. I have watched you drown yourself in anger and pain since that moment, and I want to help."

"You have been watching me? What, wait, help how?" Saul asked, confused.

"I need to ask you to do something for yourself, Saul."

"Anything for you, Emma. I will do anything to get you back."

"It's not for me, Saul. This is for you. I need you to help yourself," Emma responded.

"What do you mean?" Saul asked.

"I need you to forgive him, Saul," Emma answered.

"Forgive who, Emma?"

"Your father ..."

Saul's anger burned inside of him. How could she ask him to forgive his father? How could she even suggest that? It was his father's fault that Emma was gone in the first place.

"NO, NO. I can't. I won't," Saul said. "How could you ask me to do that, Emma? I lost everything in my life because of that man. I lost you because of him. NO,

I won't forgive that man. I will make sure I spend my life hating him because that is what he deserves."

"Saul, I love you. I don't want to see you hurt anymore. You made all those choices in your life, not your father. He hurt you, and I see the scars written all over your soul, but it is not your father's fault. It is yours. Forgive him, Saul."

Saul yelled, "NO!" and Emma was gone. Saul began to panic. "Emma? No, please don't go. Please don't go. I need you."

Saul ran around in circles, trying to find Emma again. He found nothing but more pain. He collapsed to the ground and passed out.

He woke up the next morning to being kicked. "Get up, traitor. The captain is here," a solider said.

Saul stood up, covered in mud, hay, and his own vomit. He did his best to stand at attention, but he was still hungover from the night before.

"Son, you screwed up big-time by lying to me," the captain said. "I don't like liars. I am giving you five minutes with your father to say your peace and to say good-bye."

"Say good-bye, sir?" Saul asked.

"Tonight we are going to execute him as an example to the troops that traitors are not welcome. Your father was a businessman up North and ran to the South to fight. Sounds like a traitor to me."

Saul didn't know what to say. At first, he was pleased with that news. He thought to himself, At least this time I will get to say everything I want to before he dies.

The captain continued, "That doesn't upset you, does it, son? Because if it does, I don't really care."

Saul looked up at the captain. With hatred in his eyes, he said, "Let me do it, sir."

"What did you just say to me?" The captain wasn't sure if he'd heard Saul correctly.

"I asked for your permission to let me do the execution, sir," Saul said.

The captain looked puzzled. "And why would you want to do that, son?"

"Because I hate my father, sir. I hate him more than you could possibly understand."

The captain chuckled. "You are a heartless one, son, but okay, if you insist. I will give you five minutes with him, and then we will proceed with the execution."

Saul was instructed to sit back down and wait for his father to be brought to him. Saul waited for maybe three minutes, but it felt like an eternity. What should I say to him? kept running through his mind. He had never been so anxious and worried. He looked at his hands; they were close to dripping with sweat. He felt alert and ready. His mouth dried up from all the anxiety, to the point he could barely swallow, and his heart was pounding. He was more nervous for this moment than he'd been about the battle he had just fought. He could hear the chains on his father in the distance, and he began to prepare himself. He counted the seconds until his father reached his cage. Five. He stood up. Four. He took a deep breath. Three. He cleaned himself up. Two.

He cracked his knuckles. One. He braced himself. Zero. He looked up, and there stood his father.

Chapter 10
Fighting the Wound

The cell door swung open, and the guards pushed Saul's father in. He didn't look like he was being mistreated, but he could barely lift his head off the ground, and Saul could tell that this was a conversation his father did not want to have.

A fire burned in Saul's heart. He felt nothing but hatred for this pitiful man sitting before him.

His father crawled to the farthest corner from Saul and curled up into a ball, rocking back and forth. Saul couldn't see his father's face too well, as it was mostly buried behind his knees, but he could see the lacerations and bruises from the beating Saul had given him. Saul couldn't help but smile when he saw what he had done to his father. It wasn't that he took pleasure in his father's pain, though truthfully a small part of him did, but he couldn't help but think about the symbolic nature of it all. Saul's whole life his father had inflicted deep wounds on him. His heart had always felt bruised and beaten by the actions of this man. Even after his father had "died," he still felt the pain that his father constantly inflicted on him. Saul wasn't smiling because he enjoyed seeing his father pain; he was smiling because, for the first time in Saul's life, his father knew a fraction of the pain he had been holding in his heart.

Saul sat there for what felt like an eternity without saying a word. His father was curled up in the fetal position in the corner, keeping to himself. He would lift his eyes up every couple of seconds to look at Saul, but as soon as they made eye contact, his father would jerk his head away.

Finally, Saul broke the silence. "You selfish jerk. What the hell are you doing here, in my life again? I don't need you. I don't need a father, yet here you are. What the hell are you doing down here, in the South, so far from home? We thought you were dead. Mom thought you were dead. She mourned you."

Saul's father lifted his head to listen to what Saul had to say but didn't speak a word.

"Aren't you going to say something? How about you explain to me where you were when I was trying to mask the pain you dealt me? Or better yet, why weren't you there to stop me from making your mistakes? You never got to meet my wife, the person I loved more than anything in this world. My wife killed her herself, you know? I finally found the courage to tell her that I am better than my father, that I was going to be different, that I was going to make different choices than you. I finally found the courage to tell her I screwed up and that I was cheating on her. And then she killed herself ... because of you ... you worthless man."

Saul's face turned bloodred as he spoke. In that moment, Saul knew he would have no problem killing his father, and he was just itching to do it. He was ready to end his pain, his hurt. Saul believed that everything that had gone wrong in his life was because of that man in front of him. All the hurt from losing Emma could be ended by taking this man's life, and it would be easy.

After Saul had finished speaking, there was silence. Saul's father began to weep, but still no words were spoken. Saul wanted him to explain himself—he needed to hear what pathetic excuse his father had for missing out on everything important in his son's life. Saul needed an explanation for why he was never important enough for his father. Saul sat there feeling like an angry little kid again, desperate to hear from his father. The only difference was that Saul wasn't a little kid anymore; he was a grown man who could take matters into his own hands. He felt like an angry child, but he had the anger and hatred of a man.

"Stop crying, you baby," Saul said. "I am the one who is hurting. I am the one who found out his dead father isn't dead. I am the one who should be crying, not you. What do you have to be sad about?"

Saul's father mumbled something.

"What did you just say?"

Again, he mumbled.

"I have no idea what you are trying to say. I can't hear you over there," Saul said.

Finally, his father yelled, "I said you don't know what you are talking about."

"What do you mean I don't know what I am talking about?" Saul said, filled with anger. "Who are you to tell me I don't know what I am talking about? I have suffered so much because of you, and I don't know what you are talking about?"

Saul's father sat up but continued to stare at the floor, still unable to make eye contact with his son. "You don't know anything about me. You have no idea why I am crying," his father said.

"Well, enlighten me, *Daddy*. Why are you crying?" Saul asked.

Saul's father wiped the tears from his eyes, still unable to look at his son, and simply said, "Because I am my father."

At first, Saul didn't understand what his father meant. His grandfather had passed away when Saul was only two years old, so he never had the chance to get to know him. All he knew about his grandfather was that he had raised Saul's father by himself after his wife passed away.

"Are you planning to explain, or do you expect me to just know what you mean?" Saul asked.

"I don't know how else to say it, son. I am my father," he replied.

"Okay, fine, who was your father?" Saul asked, trying to hide his interest.

"My father was not a good man. He was when he met my mother, but after she passed away, he became very angry. He was never really around—he was either working or at a bar but never at home. I remember coming home every night to an empty home, not knowing if this was the night that something was going to happen to me. I was a kid, and kids are always scared of everything. But for me, I had fought the scary monsters alone in the dark, knowing the scariest monster was coming home soon from the pub. My father beat me, Saul. Every night. He hurt me in more ways than I can tell you. I lived my whole life wounded and scared of this man. Every door that slams shut, every glass that shatters, every time someone yells, I jump. I don't think I ever told you, but I was a police officer once. I didn't last long on the force because I couldn't handle it. I just saw my father's face in every person I arrested. I grew up terrified, watching out for him everywhere I went. And what was he doing? Drinking himself to death while I suffered. Every time I fought with your mother, I found myself storming off, unable to cope. I turned to drinking just like my father. When you were born, you just never shut up, never stopped crying. As a toddler, you were so mean, especially to your mother, no matter what I did to try and teach you to be nice to others. I know it sounds silly, but you scared me, just like my dad did. So again, I turned to drinking. As business got better, I had more excuses to hide. So when I say, 'You don't know what you are talking about,' Saul, I mean that you don't understand what led me to become that 'worthless man' you call your father."

Saul almost felt sorry for his father, even though he

would never admit it. Saul knew that his father was never there for him, but at least his father never beat him, and at least he had his mother to show him love. Saul's father didn't have anyone. He didn't even have his own mother. The one person his father had in this world beat him and left him alone to wonder, Why am I not good enough? Saul began to understand that his father was a product of his upbringing, and if Saul didn't change, he would be just like him. He started to see that the wounds he felt were the same wounds his father felt. Of course, Saul was not willing to show his father compassion. The trauma of what had happened to Emma hurt more than any pain his father had caused. Saul didn't want that on himself. He was determined to make someone pay for what had happened to Emma—someone other than himself. Yet something inside of Saul needed to know more, needed to understand his father more.

"So what, am I supposed to feel sorry for you, Dad? Am I supposed to forgive what you have done to me because you weren't man enough to fight back and to stand up to your father? You are a joke, a coward. You hide behind your father like somehow it makes it okay to ruin your child's life, to ruin your own life. You blame him for all your mistakes instead of realizing that you are just a coward who's always running." Saul sat back, proud of himself for not showing this man any compassion. It felt good to stand up for himself.

His father started to chuckle.

"What is so funny, huh?" Saul asked.

"You're right, Saul. I am a coward. I do blame my

father, but if that makes me a coward, then what does that make you?"

Saul saw red. He got up and walked over to his father, got on one knee, and hit him as hard as he could over and over. The guards rushed in. Saul was ready to kill him in that moment, not only to show his father that he wasn't a coward but also because his father was right. Saul was angry at his father for blaming everything on his own dad. Yet Saul knew in his heart that he was doing the exact same thing.

The guards finally peeled Saul off his father. Two guards put their arms under his father's and had to carry him out. His head was limp, and blood dripped onto the ground.

Drip.

Drip.

Drip.

The cell door slammed shut behind them.

"Wait, please wait," Saul's father said weakly.

They stopped as his hands reached for the bars of the cell. Barely able to hold his own weight, he grabbed the bars with both hands.

"Saul, please listen to me," his father said between heavy breaths. "Please just hear me this one time."

Saul turned and punched the brick wall as hard as he could and let out a loud cry. "WHAT? ... WHAT! WHAT could you possibly have to say to me now that you couldn't have said to me while you were still my father? Before you became some lowly solider destined to be hanged? WHAT COULD YOU POSSIBLY SAY

NOW that would change anything? That would change how I feel about you? You broke me, Dad! ... You broke me ... words don't fix that. So say what you have to say, but know this." Saul paused and looked at his father while grinding his teeth. "You will be hanged for what you did to me."

Saul's father began to sob. His tears mixed with the blood from his wounds. He looked up and made eye contact with Saul for the first time since Saul was a child. With tear- and blood-soaked eyes, he looked at Saul and said, "Please, Saul, don't become your father. Please, Saul, forgive me. Don't make my mistakes; don't hold on to the pain. Don't become me. Break the cycle." His head dropped, and the guards dragged him away.

Saul was left with a choice: Do I forgive, or do I hate? His father was never there for him, never around to help him grow up and learn how to be a man. As far as Saul was concerned, he never had a father. So why should he be forgiven? "An eye for an eye," right? Yet the decision wasn't that simple. Yes, his father had hurt him. Yes, his father was never there to pick up the pieces that he had broken. But his father could say the same thing.

In that moment, Saul remembered the last words Emma left him with in his cell: *Saul, I love you. I don't want to see you hurt anymore. You made all those choices in your life, not your father. He hurt you, and I see the scars written all over your soul, but it is not your father's fault. It is yours. Forgive him, Saul.*

Maybe Emma knew. Maybe Emma knew that his

father was only acting out of his own pain, out of his own wound. *Forgive him, Saul.* The words kept running through his mind, but how? He couldn't let go of the pain and shame he felt from Emma's death. Every time he thought of forgiving his father, he couldn't help but think that if it weren't for him, Emma would still be here. I miss her so much, Saul kept thinking.

"I need you, Emma. Please talk to me. Please just tell me it is okay to forgive him. Please just tell me that I didn't lose you because of my father. I know I made my own mistakes, but they were influenced by him. If he had been around, I would have never cheated on you, and you would still be here. Emma, please just say something to me."

He yelled to Heaven, praying Emma would say something, but he heard nothing. Not even a whisper. All he had were the words Emma left him with: *Forgive him, Saul.*

Chapter 11
Do I Forgive?

As I listened to Vivek tell the story, I couldn't help but feel like I was a part of it. I understood, to a small degree, the cycle of anger that Saul was going through. It made me think of the passion and anger I had inside.

I didn't hate my father in the least—that was not what I meant. But I did hate what I saw whenever I looked at myself in the mirror, and oftentimes, I ended up blaming my dad for that. Every time I took my shirt off, I saw some chubby, fat kid, some kid who wasn't worth anyone's attention or affection. Whose fault was that, though? When I truly asked myself that question, the blame oddly never fell on me. I never took the steps to better myself. I blamed the bullies in school or my dad for always making his stupid jokes or pushing me to lose more weight.

I had a lot of self-esteem issues, and maybe my circumstances had a lot to do with it. I was bullied, I was beat up, and yes, my father had said a lot of things that had hurt me and stuck with me over the years. But why was I acting like Saul and not taking responsibility for my problems? They were *my* circumstances, my problems. How could I break the cycle of anger that I seemed to be perpetuating?

I knew my father loved me. Clearly, he could see how much I hated the way I looked, and he had heard the stories of the bullies at school and had tried to help. He tried to get me to work out and created a diet plan for me, yet for some reason, those things just made me feel worse about myself. I wished I could talk to him about that, but I didn't want to upset him. Did that mean he deserved the blame for my low self-esteem? At the end of the day, they were still my circumstances, my problems. It wasn't his body that needed changing.

The story Vivek told gave me a new perspective though. Seeing the pain Saul's father went through made me realize that maybe my dad had gone through the same thing—maybe he was hurt and wounded by the mistakes of his own father.

I began to realize why Vivek was telling us this story. I had been blaming my father for things that were in my control. I needed to break the cycle of anger.

The things that bothered me about my dad were from him not breaking the cycle of pain caused by his own father. Much like Saul's father in the story, my grandfather had not been a good man. He had been an abusive drunk who left my father when he was just a young boy. It was until later in life that my father learned that he was found dead on a beach, probably around sixty. So many years passed without knowing his father.

My dad had an amazing mother. She raised several kids on her own, and she struggled financially, so much so that she had to place my father and his siblings in foster care for some time. My father said that was probably the saddest moment of his life. Luckily, though, when things became more stable, his mother was able to get them back. My dad's childhood wasn't easy, and he had to figure out most of life's troubles on his own. He never had a chance to confront his father and understand what had made his father the way he was. When I thought of it like that, I realized how strong of a man my father really was. It also made me realize how selfish it was to hold on to such anger, and how wrong it was to blame my father for what I saw in the mirror. It seemed childish, considering what my father had been through.

As I thought about all of this, I found myself crying.

"Are you all right, Ezra? What's wrong?" Vivek asked.

I wiped at my tears. "Nothing, man. I am just thinking about things."

"Anything you want to share or talk about? The story is almost done. We can take a break."

I could tell Vivek sensed the gears turning in my head, and I knew he wouldn't let this go without me saying something.

"I just wish Saul knew his grandfather," I said. "Forgiving his father wouldn't be so hard if Saul knew who his father's father was ... does that make sense?"

"That's right, Ezra," Vivek said. "It's not easy to forgive something you don't understand. For Saul, he had no context, just a bunch of words. He never saw his father get beat, and he never saw his grandfather drunk. All he ever saw was his father being absent. He never saw his father's wounds. He only ever saw the side effects—the aftermath."

My tears continued to fall as I thought about the wounds my father had carried throughout his life, and it gave me a lot of respect for him. My wounds were still there, but they just seemed so small in comparison, and it was clear to me that I was in control of them, that I could make a difference.

I realized I was lucky to have a father I could run home to. My father, Saul, and Daniel—none of them had that opportunity. My dad never had a "Vivek" come and challenge the things that he felt. In that moment, I really wished my dad was there with me next to the fire. I wanted to tell him how great of a man I really thought he was. I didn't know if anyone had ever told him "good job," that despite everything the world threw at him, he turned out to be an amazing man. I wished there was cell reception so that I could reach him; he deserved to know that all those years of pain turned out to be worth it. He deserved to know that he was loved and appreciated.

Vivek gave all of us a moment of silence to ponder everything that he had been talking about. After a minute or two, he broke the silence.

"You guys ready to finish up the story?" Vivek

asked.

"Yeah," we all answered with a dread-filled tone, expecting the ending of the story to be even more depressing than what we'd already heard.

"Cheer up, guys. I know this story is kinda heavy, but I promise it will be worth it. Plus, there is a huge plot twist at the end."

As soon as Daniel and Jordan heard *plot twist*, they were back in the game. For me, I didn't know if my mind could take any more twists and bending.

"So, did I leave off with Saul sitting in the cell, debating his choices?" Vivek asked.

"Yeah, he was just remembering what Emma had said," Daniel replied.

"Oh, okay, right. So Saul sat there, remembering that Emma had told him he needed to forgive his father but also forgive himself. Saul wasn't sure how though. He wanted to believe what his father had told him, and he wanted to forgive him, but to Saul, his father's absence in his life killed Emma. Could you forgive someone who killed the love of your life? I think deep down Saul knew that his father wasn't responsible for Emma's death, but the grief was still too real to come to grips with that. Saul needed to blame someone. He had no reason to forgive. And you are right, Ezra, Saul never knew his grandfather, so to him, his father could just be desperate to save his own life. Saul was faced with a choice: Does he forgive, or does he continue to hate?"

Chapter 12
The Bird Is Free

As Saul walked around his cell anxiously, his captain came up to the cell door. "Son, what is wrong with you? Can you tell me that? Who told you to beat one of my prisoners? I don't care who he is, even if he is your father, you don't touch one of my prisoners unless I tell you to. You best get that through that thick skull of yours real fast, son. Now, are you still wanting to do this?"

Saul knew his captain was referring to the execution. "Yes, sir. I want that man to pay for what he has done."

"Well, I am not going to act like I know what that means, and I honestly don't care. But there you have it, boys." The captain looked at his guards and pointed at Saul. "We got ourselves an executioner and an undertaker—you get to bury him, too, by the way."

The captain never skipped a beat. He didn't like the fact that they were putting a man to death to make an example, but he needed to show strength to his army. Saul could see in his eyes he hated the idea of Saul killing his own father, but Saul had volunteered. Name a better way to show the urgency for dedication to the captain and his leadership than killing his own father. It was a symbolic picture that his men needed. So despite the captain's moral dilemma, he let the show go on.

"Wear this," the captain said, signaling one of the guards to hand Saul a pile of clothes. "I can't have you going in front of my army covered in mud, blood, and tears. Take this bucket, clean yourself off, and put that clean uniform on. And, son, wash your hands too. You look like a goddamn savage." The captain walked away and left a guard to wait for Saul.

Saul knelt down next to the bucket to clean the mud off. The cold water felt good on all the cuts on his hands. He felt like he'd broken his hand after punching the wall. He took his time cleaning off the blood. It was a strange feeling for Saul. Though he was determined to take his father's life, the debate still wasn't over in his mind. Should I forgive him, or should I hate him? was the question that seemed to have no answer. Saul knew if he changed his mind now, his captain would have them both killed. He also knew if he decided not to kill his father that he would regret the decision forever. He needed to blame someone for losing Emma. He needed to blame someone for his mistakes. Saul didn't know what to do.

As he continued to clean himself up, he said a quick prayer: "If you send Emma, I could really use her help. I am struggling, God. I hate my father for the things that he has done, but I know he only did what his father did to him. I need to find peace, but I don't know how. If I kill him, I don't think I will ever find peace. If I let him live and forgive him, I don't think I can let go of the grief I have over Emma. I am so lost. I am alone. Make my decision clear."

Saul finished cleaning himself up and put on his uniform.

"Guard, I am ready," Saul said as he walked to the front of the cell.

"You sure you want to do this? I have issues with my father, too, but kill him? Really?" the guard said to Saul. "I just don't understand."

Saul looked at him. "He was never a father to me. Whether it's right or wrong, I blame him for everything that has gone wrong in my life, and one of us needs to pay."

The guard looked at Saul like he was crazy, and honestly, at that point, Saul was crazy. He just needed something to end—something to be put to rest. The guard opened the door and took Saul by the arm. The guard walked him to the front of the barracks, and there stood everyone from his platoon. All the men he had gotten close to were there, standing together, ready for him to execute his father. It was all so surreal. In the cell, Saul was ready to do it, but it hadn't seemed real in there. It hadn't seemed like it was really going to happen. He took a deep breath and started walking down the center of the crowd to the tree where his father was tied. Saul's mind was racing, but on the outside he looked cold and heartless. You would swear by the look on his face that he had been waiting his whole life for this moment. In a lot of ways, that was how it felt for Saul. He'd been waiting for closure. He'd been waiting for the wound to heal. How the wound would heal was a mystery to Saul, something his brain still had not figured out. It was time to decide though.

The captain stood at the base of the tree next to Saul's father and watched every step that Saul took, secretly hoping Saul would change his mind. But Saul was determined to move forward, hoping an alternative would become clear.

"Either you make it very clear I need to forgive my father, or I will kill him," he kept muttering as a prayer under his breath. Every step he took, he was more determined to just end it all. With every step, he left a little bit more of the idea to forgive his father behind.

As Saul made his way through the crowd to the tree before him, he saw an eagle fly overhead. He couldn't help but watch the beautiful, majestic bird open its wings and glide through the air with gentle ease. The bird was free. As he watched the eagle, he was in a trance and no longer stuck in this awful situation. Then Saul remembered once more what Emma had said: *Saul, I love you. I don't want to see you hurt anymore ... Forgive him, Saul.* In that moment, he realized a profound truth. He looked at the men standing around, and all he saw was pain and suffering. Every single man standing there was holding on to some wound, some life-long emotional affliction. He looked back at the eagle. The reason the bird was so free was because it wasn't holding on to anything. If the bird were carrying a heavy weight on its back, it would go nowhere; it wouldn't be able to fly.

Saul looked at his father, who was on his knees with his head down and sweat dripping off his forehead. He was in bondage. Literally, yes, but he was also stuck with the pain and suffering of what his father had done to him. Just like himself. In that moment, it was clear to Saul what freedom, joy, and happiness meant. It meant no longer carrying a heavy weight on his back. It meant being free of anger and suffering so that he could be like the bird he was watching—free from bondage, free from suffering. The question was, How? All of that was much easier said than done. Their burdens were already breaking their backs. All of these thoughts ran through Saul's mind as he approached his father.

It came time to decide. As Saul walked up to the tree, he was handed the opening of a noose. The captain took a step forward to address the troops. Saul held the noose in his hands while the captain spoke.

"Gentlemen, it's with a severely heavy heart that I condemn this man to death. As many of you have heard, this man ... is Saul Treeborn's father. For reasons beyond my understanding, Saul has volunteered to execute this man. This man is guilty of the following: treason against the United States of America and crimes against humanity. Treason is punishable by death. Let this be an example to every man standing here today—your allegiance lies with me and the United States of America, in that order. This man is Saul's father, but just as Saul is demonstrating, I demand your allegiance."

Everyone looked at Saul like he was the poster boy of the army. Before the captain had spoken, everyone had looked at Saul with disgust about what he was about to do, but now, everyone was looking up to Saul like he was some kind of hero. Saul didn't like the pressure. Honestly, this had nothing to do with the captain, the war, or anyone but Saul and his father. His allegiance wasn't with the captain at all. What he was about to do was purely for selfish reasons.

Saul looked down at the noose in his hands and felt dirty. Suddenly he felt sick. He was about to take a man's life simply because he carried an open wound. He was his father.

"Mr. Treeborn," the captain said to Saul's father, "do you have any last words that you would like to share with your son?"

His father began to sob. "I don't want to die. I am not ready," he said, stuttering on each word.

The captain's eyes softened briefly, then he turned to Saul. "Saul, are you ready?"

"I am ready," Saul replied.

The captain handed him a black bag, and Saul slipped it over his father's head. Saul then took the noose and slipped it over his father's head and began to tighten it around his neck. Saul asked the two guards next to his father to place him on the horse. All Saul had to do now was throw the other end of the rope over the branch and tie it off. Everything was set in motion. Saul's heart began to race faster than he ever knew was possible. He was panicking and everyone could see it. What do I do? I can't kill this man, but he killed Emma. This is your father! You can't kill your father. But you need to kill him. His head filled with arguments and pleas for help.

He was lost.

He was scared.

He looked up to the sky, hoping for a sign, but all he saw was the eagle lurking above, almost taunting Saul with this idea of freedom. Saul so desperately wanted to be free, to let go of this bondage, to break the cycle of pain and suffering. He didn't want to be angry anymore. He wanted to know what joy felt like and what it felt like to wake up happy again. He wanted the pain to be over and the wound to be healed. Saul closed his eyes. He prayed to himself: give me freedom.

When Saul opened his eyes, he knew that his father was looking at him through the black hood, ready for what was next. Saul was about to smack the horse on the rear, causing it to run away and his father to hang, but then he was interrupted.

"Wait!" he heard a woman's voice say. Saul stopped before he could hit the horse.

"What are you doing, son?" the captain asked Saul.

"You didn't hear that? Sounded like a woman yelled, 'Wait.'"

Everyone looked at Saul like he was crazy.

"It has been dead silent, son. You are losing your mind," the captain said.

Saul looked out into the crowd, trying to find the

woman who yelled for him to wait but saw only men. He walked back to the horse and began to pet its head. Everyone looked at Saul like he had completely gone insane. He heard the woman's voice again.

"Saul, wait!"

"Who is that? Show yourself! Who keeps yelling?" Saul screamed into the crowd.

"Son, you clearly can't do this. Guards, take Saul away." The captain motioned for the guards.

"No, I can do this. I need to do this!" Saul exclaimed, rushing back to the horse. He heard the woman again but ignored her, focusing on the task at hand. Right as he got into position again, Saul's father turned his head toward Saul.

"Saul, I need to tell you something," said his father.

"It is too late, Dad. You can't stop me. You deserve this," Saul said, tears rolling down his cheeks.

"Saul, please wait. You need to hear this. Just wait one second."

Saul repeatedly kicked the tree and pulled at his hair like a crazy man. He grabbed his father's shirt and pulled him down slightly so that he was next to his father's head.

"What do I need to hear? What are you going to tell me? You are sorry? ... that you love me? Is that somehow going to help me forgive you?" Then Saul got a strange whiff of perfume that was coming off his father. Something was so familiar about that scent, but he couldn't place it.

And then it hit him—that perfume was the same

scent Emma had worn on their wedding day.

Sobbing, Saul scrambled to take the noose off his father's head. He pulled his father to the ground to make sense of what was happening. No one stopped him. They watched in amazement at the drama that was unfolding.

"Where did you get that perfume? Why are you wearing it? Why are you doing this to me? Why?" Saul was panicking. "Did Emma talk to you too? Please, Dad, how did you get that perfume?" Saul fell on his bottom, taking his father down with him.

Everyone was looking at Saul as he tried to sniff this man; it looked like Saul had lost it completely. The smell was so real to him, like Emma was standing right there.

"I miss her, Dad. I miss her so much. I know you never met her, but she was the most beautiful woman in the world. Her hair was curly with this burnt-red color when the sun hit it. She had these beautiful freckles that covered her cheeks. My favorite thing in the world would be to kiss her cheekbones; she would just smile and push her head into my shoulder. Dad, you would never forget how beautiful her eyes were. They were hazel, but if I ever made her feel extra special, they would get a darker-green hue to them, almost like fresh pine trees in May. Gosh, I'll never forget how she looked on our wedding day. She was so beautiful. Her eyes were green the whole honeymoon too! That only happened when she felt overwhelmed with love. I miss her, Dad. I miss her touch and her smell. I miss her so much. Where did you get that perfume, Dad? Please, Dad, where did you get that perfume?" Saul had officially given up on looking sane. At this point, he was resting his head on his father, just trying to get another whiff of Emma's perfume.

"It's your fault I lost her, Dad. It is your fault. You killed her. Why, Dad? Why did you make me like this? Why didn't you stop me? I hate you. I hate you. I hate you," he said while hitting his father with what little strength he had left.

"Son, come here," his father said.

Saul moved over to his father's face. His father took a deep breath, and the words that came out of his mouth were not his own.

"Forgive him, Saul," in Emma's voice was what Saul heard from underneath the black hood, but it was impossible. The voice went on. "Saul, I love you. I don't want to see you hurt anymore. You made all those choices in your life, not your father ... forgive him, Saul."

Saul ripped the black hood off his father's head and gasped. Saul crawled backward as fast as he could, but his back hit the tree. He closed his eyes, hoping what he saw wasn't real.

"This isn't real. This isn't real. This isn't real," he kept telling himself. With his eyes closed and people whispering all around him, all Saul could hear was Emma's voice saying, "Forgive him, Saul. Forgive him."

Saul finally opened his eyes, but what he saw didn't go away.

There he was, looking at himself. Saul was looking at himself.

Chapter 13
The Plot Twist

I knew Vivek had said there was going to be a plot twist, but he didn't say there would be five plot twists in one. I looked around the fire at Daniel and Jordan; their mouths were wide-open.

"That would be the trippiest movie ever!" Daniel exclaimed.

Vivek laughed. "The *trippiest*? Is that a word?"

Daniel laughed. "Well, what word would you use? I mean, that was pretty crazy, man."

Everyone was laughing except for me. The story felt so real. Vivek had told it with such emotion, but now, knowing how it all ended, there was no way that it was true. Unless they had shape-shifting, perfume-wearing crazy people back in the 1800s. The story didn't mean anything if it was all fake.

"So none of that was real, was it?" I asked Vivek.

"What do you think, Ezra? Do you think it was a true story?"

"Well, of course not. There is no way that last part could be true." I wasn't really sure what he was getting at, to be honest. He couldn't convince me that any of that was real.

"A little while ago, you were crying about what was in the story. Fiction or not, stories hold so much power in our lives. They can speak so much truth into our lives. Why does this story have to be fake?" Vivek asked.

I was confused. "The tears weren't fake, but I was comparing my struggles with Saul's. If Saul is fiction, then it is no better than comparing myself to Batman."

"That was the point of the story, Ezra. I wanted you to put yourself in Saul's shoes and understand his pain. We all have wounds," Vivek said. "For example, Daniel, your dad was never around, so you can understand the pain Saul was talking about. Jordan, your parents are dealing with an affair, so you can understand the pain that Saul and Emma went through. And Ezra, you are angry at others for how you see yourself, so you can understand how Saul feels when he doesn't own up to his problems. It is more than just a story. We are all hurting in one way or another, and we should learn from the mistakes of others. We need to understand that Saul's story is your story ... it is my story."

I understood what Vivek was saying, but it just didn't seem right. This story had really gotten to me. I could swear that I was looking at Saul's face as Vivek told the story. It just seemed so real.

"I guess you're right, Vivek," I said. "The story doesn't have to be real to have a real effect on us."

"Wait a second," Vivek responded abruptly. "I never said it wasn't real. I said the point of the story was to get you to think, but the story is real."

I felt like Vivek was playing with me, like this was some bad joke that he was determined to get us to laugh about.

"Vivek, it can't be real," I said.

"Why, Ezra? Don't you remember I said that there was a plot twist?"

The three of us looked at one another in confusion.

Jordan spoke up. "Wait, I thought you already did the plot twist."

Vivek just laughed. "No, all that craziness at the end of the story was just the story. That wasn't the plot twist."

"So what is the plot twist?" I exclaimed, almost angrily. I honestly didn't know what to think. Vivek arched his back to get something out of his back pocket. He sat back down and unfolded his wallet and took out a plastic card.

"This is my driver's license from four years ago. Don't freak out. I will explain everything, but this is the plot twist." Vivek passed his license around the circle, starting with Jordan.

Jordan's jaw dropped, and then he just started laughing. "No freaking way, man."

Then Daniel followed suit. "You tricked us, man. That was sneaky."

"What are you guys going on about? Let me see," I said, reaching for the card. Daniel handed me the card, and I couldn't believe what I was seeing. On the left was a picture of Vivek. The card listed his hair color as brown. Brown eyes. 205 pounds. Height 6'1". Organ donor. All normal information, but at the bottom left-hand side of his driver's license, right under his picture, it said:

Saul Treeborn. 525 Colored Wind Ave., New York, New York, 10014.

Chapter 14
What's Your Name?

"Wait a second. *You* are Saul Treeborn? Why does everyone call you Vivek?" I asked. Daniel and Jordan were still laughing their butts off because they had gotten tricked, but I was angry. I didn't understand how they weren't upset about this. I had gotten emotionally invested in the story that Vivek—I mean, Saul—was telling us. I really felt for Saul, you know? I had put myself in his shoes, and it turned out this guy was just making up the story about himself. The story had to be made up.

"What's your deal, man?" I asked. "Why did you take us all the way out here to tell us some 'true' story and trick us? I don't get it," I said, putting the word *true* in air quotes.

Vivek seemed burdened by what I had said. He really took it to heart that I'd said his story wasn't true, almost like I was telling him that his pain didn't matter. I wanted to believe the story, but the more I thought about it, the more skeptical I became. I looked across the fire and saw Vivek on the verge of tears. There had to be more to this story.

"Just tell us what's up, man. Why were you crying earlier, and why do you keep saying this story is true?" I asked.

Vivek stared into the fire with sadness written all over his face. It took him a few seconds to answer me.

"As you can see, my birth name was Saul Treeborn the Second. I was born in New York. My father was Saul Treeborn Senior, and I actually married the love of my life, Emma Grace. Man, were we happy. We loved each other more than you will ever understand. But I screwed up. I got so caught up with hating my father and trying to mask my pain with alcohol that I slept with my sectary, Jill. The one person I loved more than anyone else in this world killed herself because I screwed up. So I say that story is true, Ezra, because it is. It's my story. It is the story of how I found my name."

Vivek looked down at a picture in his wallet. I couldn't see it, but I figured it must have been of Emma.

"Is that Emma?" I asked with sorrow in my voice, trying to make up for lashing out.

Vivek nodded. "This is a picture she took for me before our wedding. She didn't want us to see each other until she was walking down the aisle, so she took this picture to calm my nerves."

He passed it around to all of us. It put a face to the pain we were seeing in Vivek.

"She's really beautiful, Vivek. You were a lucky man," Daniel said.

"I am a lucky man, Daniel."

"So why tell your story through a made-up story wrapped in a historical event?" I asked Vivek, trying not to get tongue-tied by my own question.

"Short answer, men have always learned best through stories. Most of our written history was transmitted verbally for hundreds of years. Also, I was a history teacher before all this, so as a tribute to my old life, I try to give you a little history lesson while we are out here. That is why I throw those dates in there," Vivek said with half a smile and a brief, sad chuckle. "Long answer, I told my story through the Civil War because that is exactly what was happening in my life. I was fighting against myself. I was constantly blaming my father for my mistakes. Constantly wrapping myself, my identity, up in my circumstances and the things that I couldn't control. To break the cycle of pain and suffering in my life, to find my new name, I had go to war with myself." He pounded his fist to his chest.

Something inside of me understood. The pain that Vivek had faced in his life wasn't pointless if he could save us from the same pain and learn from his mistakes. He was trying to help us find meaning.

"Jordan, what does your name mean?" Vivek asked.

"Um, I don't know. I always figured I was named after Michael Jordan. My folks love basketball."

Vivek wasn't laughing anymore. "No. Your name in English means 'river of judgment,' but in Hebrew it means 'to flow down.' The Jordan is a river in the Middle East and was a huge theme in the biblical narrative. Let me ask you something, What does a river always do?"

"It flows?" Jordan answered.

"Exactly, Jordan. It always flows. You aren't named after some basketball player; your name isn't some copy of greatness. You are Jordan. You are constant, always flowing, always faithful. You are powerful, and if people cross your path, you are a force to be reckoned with. You can be chaotic and majestic at the same time, but most importantly, when someone learns who you are and understands your name, they learn you can be gentle. There will be a woman who will come along one day, Jordan, and she will take the time to learn who you are, and I promise you, you will learn to be gentle. Be chaotic, but never stop flowing. You are Jordan, always faithful."

Then Vivek turned to me. "Now, Ezra, what does your name mean?"

I had no idea what to say. Everything Vivek had just told Jordan felt right. I looked over at Jordan. He sat with a puffed-up chest and tears in his eyes just like Daniel had earlier that day. But what did my name mean? I wanted to answer Vivek, but I was afraid that I would find out my name meant "weak." Or "gay." Or "pathetic." My identity was wrapped up in what the world had told me about myself. All I knew was how I felt: scared and alone.

Just like Jordan had, it was easy for me to come up with some lame explanation of my name. Maybe my parents had met a nice guy named Ezra once, I thought to myself, trying to find an excuse as to why my name might mean anything more than "child."

"Well, what do you think, Ezra? What does it mean?" Vivek asked again.

Tears filled my eyes. "It means 'child.' It means 'weak ... pathetic, little boy.'"

Vivek's eyes welled up with tears. "No, son, it doesn't mean 'weak.' You are powerful and strong. Ezra is another historical Jewish character, one of the Old Testament prophets. When everyone was going back to Jerusalem to rebuild the temple, Ezra spent the time rebuilding the hearts of the people. He was the guy who stood in front of a crowd and stirred the passions of others. People usually say that Ezra means 'helper,' and that is right, but there is so much more to that name. The verb *azaz* in Hebrew is often used in conjunction with Ezra. *Azaz* means 'strong' or 'powerful.' Do you get what I am trying to say, Ezra? Your name means 'powerful.' Your name means 'helper.' Your name means 'compassionate.' You, my friend, are the strongest of warriors. In the Torah, your name is described as a bird of prey. When men see you, Ezra, they see a warrior that is freed from struggles in this life. Not because you don't go through them—no, they see a warrior that is free because you have learned how to fly. You are the strongest of warriors because you are not tied to this ground. You have beauty and compassion written on the very core of your heart, and you invoke passion in people when they see you. Your name does not mean 'child.' Your name does not mean 'weak.'

Your name is a bird of prey. Majestic and beautiful but a warrior that is unmatched."

Vivek was standing up and practically yelling. His face was covered in tears, and there was passion in his voice. He needed me to know that my name was more than my wounds. He needed me to know that I was not my pain. He needed me to learn from his mistakes. It was clear to me now why Vivek brought us here to talk about names; it was because the mistakes he had made were because he never knew who he was.

Vivek had gone through life just figuring things out as he went along. His identity became a mirror of wherever he found himself in life, whether it be married, at work, or angry at his dad. His identity reflected his surroundings. Vivek needed me to understand that my name, my identity, was independent of whatever anyone said about me and that it was what I thought about myself. I was so much more than my insecurities.

"Do you understand, Ezra? I mean, do you understand the power that is in your name?" Vivek asked me while I was still wrestling with my thoughts.

"Yeah, I think I understand. I am not weak just because I feel weak. I am not my pain. I am strong."

Vivek walked around the fire and stuck his hand out. "Nice to meet you, Ezra." He did the same to both Jordan and Daniel, and in that moment we could have fought a war. We all felt like mighty warriors who had just been given their mission, their purpose.

Something was still bothering me though. It was great that we had found our names, but what about

Vivek? How did he find his name? The name Vivek was a lot different from the name Saul.

"Why Vivek?" I asked.

Everyone looked at me like I had ruined the mood.

"Why the name Vivek? What does your name mean?" I asked with a serious tone in my voice.

"Well, Ezra, let me tell you."

Chapter 15
Discerning Wisdom

Do not go gentle into that good night,
Rage, rage against the dying of the light.

Vivek recited a poem to us. "It was written by a man named Dylan Thomas, who died in 1953," he said. "'Do not go gentle into that good night.'"

"Wait, you are saying a poem gave you your new name?" Daniel asked.

"I will explain. This poem helped me start my journey into finding my name," Vivek said. "After I lost Emma, I went into a deep depression and began drinking all the time. I got into a lot of fights and got into trouble with the law. I had lost my job as a history teacher because I showed up to work drunk. I had lost everything. I wanted to die. I wanted to be free of suffering, but I didn't know where to start. The only time I felt something was at the end of a bottle. I hated everything. It was a very dark time in my life.

"One night I got into a bar fight and got the crap beaten out of me—just like in the story I told you boys earlier. The police officer who came and took care of the fight immediately recognized my name from my ID and knew who my father was. I was shocked to find out that this officer was my father's old partner. At that time, I never even knew that my father had been a police officer. I don't think my father was hiding that from me; we just never talked about his past much. What are the chances of that in New York City? The one officer who picked me up that night was the one officer who was my father's partner. At the time, it just seemed like a really odd coincidence, and hell, maybe it was just that, but that was when the journey to find my name started.

"In the story I told you, I said that the officer gave me a choice: either go to jail or join the military. In reality, the choice wasn't that. I remember that night clearly because it changed my whole life.

"'You are a joke, Saul,' the officer said to me. 'Your father was someone in this world. He made a name for himself. Yeah, he left his friends behind, but he did it so that people would know his name. I liked your father, but you—you're just another drunk. If it weren't for your father, I would just take you to jail and that would be that. But I am going to give you an option, Saul, a choice. The bartender wants to press charges. I can let the bartender press charges and take you to jail, or you can agree to go to rehab right now. Not tomorrow or in an hour. You pack your bags right now, and I take you to rehab. So, what will it be?'

"I remember feeling scared, terrified actually, and not knowing what to do. If I said yes to the officer's offer, I would be admitting there was a problem that needed to be fixed. I would be admitting that I had been hiding from my shame and guilt. Ultimately, I would be admitting that my actions might have caused Emma's death. If I didn't take his offer, I would go to jail, and even though it probably wouldn't be for long, I would be stuck with my shame and guilt without any way of dealing with it. I would have to sober up. I wouldn't have any booze or anyone willing to help me through it, and when I got out, I would be the same. I would go further and further down the hole I'd dug for myself.

"I eventually decided to take the offer and go to rehab. I didn't join the military and find my father on a literal battlefield like the Saul in the story, but that story wasn't made up. I found my father on the battlefield of my mind, of my soul, and it turned out it was me the whole time. In rehab, I was forced to give up any substance I was using, and I had to be completely sober. Since Emma was gone and my mother had no idea where I was, I never had any visitors. I was very alone. I was trapped. The staff there forced me to deal with Emma's death and forced me to replay that event over and over again. I had to go to counseling five days a week and group meetings three times a week. I can't remember another time that I have been forced to struggle with my problems so much and forced to grow.

"Everyone in my rehab center had to share a room with someone else to keep one another accountable. I slept closest to the door. Through the small window on our door, I could see a poem on the wall in the hallway. I couldn't see the whole thing from my bed, just a few lines: 'Do not go gentle into that good night' and 'Rage, rage against the dying of the light.' From day one there was something that was just odd about this poem to me, something that was touching my very core. Every night before I fell asleep, I would stare at those lines of the poem and whisper them to myself. At the time, I did not know what the poem meant, and there was so much on my mind that I never really sat down and thought about its meaning. But I knew that it had something to do with holding life precious. This was my first introduction to the idea of impermanence that I told you about earlier. I went to bed every night reading these lines of this poem and hoping that I would wake up with the desire to live, the desire to love life again in spite of the 'dying of the light.'

"The program itself was five months, and by the time I was three months into it, I had made very little progress. The doctor and staff had been making me talk about Emma and who I blamed for her death. Obviously, I blamed my father for her death. I blamed him for not being there to help me be a better man. I told the staff that I would never forgive a man who abandoned his family and left them with so much pain. The staff kept pushing me to understand that the situation that led to Emma's death was due to my choices. But I would not believe them. I needed someone to blame. I was very prideful and didn't believe

I needed help.

"One morning I woke up in a panic. All the conversations about Emma were making me dream about that terrible night. I would see myself walking into that room of our house again and again where she and Jill sat. I could feel Emma's lips on my face, and I would wake up to the loud bang every morning. When I went to counseling that morning, I broke down for the first time in three months. I spilled my heart to the doctor and told him everything that I was thinking.

"I told him about the dreams I was having about Emma and how I hated myself for what I did to her. I told him how I stilled blamed my father but that I couldn't forgive myself either. I told him that I was broken. Hurting. Sick. For the first time in three months, I felt like I was actually working through my issues and my pain. This progress stayed steady for a few weeks, and then everything changed.

"After a group session and dinner one night, I walked the length of the cold hallway back to my room. I lay down and turned off the lights. The lights in the hallway were always on, and I could still read part of that poem. It had become kind of a nightly prayer for me. I would lie down and look at that poem and try to understand it, try to make it my own. On this night, I found myself saying my first prayer in a long time.

"I prayed, 'God, I don't really know what to say to you. You don't seem to be around very much. I seem to almost have an anger and bitterness toward you like I do my father. Why didn't you stop her? Why did you leave me here alone to die? I don't understand ... the only difference between you and my father is that you knew Emma. You knew the amazing woman she was. You know how sad and blank this world has become without her. My father didn't. Help me find color in my life again. Help me come to peace with Emma's absence. I don't want her death to be in vain.'

"I looked once more at the poem through the window and saw that it was urging me to rage. It dawned on me that I needed to go to war with myself. It finally clicked that the reason rehab hadn't been working wasn't because my light had already died, but it was because I wasn't willing to do what I needed to do to change. I needed to rage against myself, rage against the dying of the light. This realization allowed me to peel the hardened layers of my heart back and expose the wound that I was holding onto.

"You see, boys, I told you that the story wasn't fiction because it isn't. Yes, I added dates and some details to the story to get you interested, to help you remember the emotion of the story, but it doesn't mean it was fake. I chose the Civil War for a reason, because that is what I am asking you to do. Maybe the wound is small and easy to live with. For men like me, maybe the wound is deep and gushing blood our whole lives. These wounds aren't closed by throwing on a Band-Aid and just sucking it up; that is society's solution, and it clearly doesn't work. That is the answer most men stick with, and we can see the effects of it throughout history. We can't heal without first closing the wound. The wound is healed through closure.

"The story says a lot about where my heart was and who I am as a man. I was trying to fight the outcomes of my mistakes by blaming my father. I came to the battlefield thirsty for revenge. Yet when I finally had it, when my father was on that horse, ready to be hanged, and I took the hood off ... it was me the whole time. I was fighting myself. The Civil War wasn't between my father and me; it was between me and myself. Yes, my dad was never there for me, and it hurt, but I took his mistakes and wore them as my identity. Every mistake, every action, and every character trait I showed the world was cloaked in this reality that 'Daddy wasn't there.' My father became my name, and I never realized who I was as a man. Boys, if I could give you one piece of advice, it would be this. Let the battle rage. I spent my whole life trying to meet my father on the battlefield, but it wasn't until I met myself there that I became whole.

"We weren't created to perpetually make the same mistakes over and over again. yet that is what we find ourselves doing. We need to declare war. But when you don't know why you fight, you end up fighting for the wrong things. Looking throughout history, you will see that not many wars were fought for noble causes. Most bloodshed comes between small groups of men who disagree with one another about some nonessential of life, usually money or greed. There is nothing noble about that kind of war. Fighting for your identity, waging a war against yourself to break the chains of the past— that is noble. The mistakes of others often lock us into an identity that is not our own. That is why we must declare a civil war.

"These wounds we hold onto, boys, tell us that we aren't good enough. But men were meant to be mighty. Mighty in the sense that we have the chance to be free. We don't have to be what anyone says we are."

Chapter 16
Stop Climbing for Bananas

"You never told us how you got your name, Vivek. I mean, you told us what the story was about, but that didn't explain how you went from Saul to Vivek," I said.

Vivek chuckled. "You're right, Ezra. Do you remember that poem I said I could see from my bedroom window?"

"Yeah, we remember," Daniel said on behalf of the group.

"After rehab, I spent a lot of time thinking about things. I was trying to avoid sliding back into depression and addiction, so I made sure I was busy. I got a small apartment and a new job, and I started saving my money, hoping to make a better life for myself. I took those words from that poem and painted them on my wall as a reminder to fight for meaning. Fight for life. Fight against the dying of the light. But I still didn't feel better. I was just wasting away, waiting desperately for something to change. I had forgotten how to live. I had forgotten what life was. I wasn't depressed like I was when I went into rehab, but I wasn't living.

"After rehab, I started work for a call center. I was only there for about two months when I realized that something needed to change, that I needed to learn how to live again. I called my boss, and I quit over the phone. I took my retirement money out of my 401(k) and took out all the money I had in savings. I sat down and planned my trip to find meaning in my life. I booked three tickets for a six-month trip. The first ticket was to India, and I was planning to stay there for three months. The second was from India to Israel, where I would spend the remaining three months, and the last ticket was to come back home.

"A week later, it was time to board my plane to India. I was heading to a wellness center in southern India. They offered a place of healing and meditation. They had classes on yoga and how to reach your inner person. But what interested me the most was that they would teach me Kalaripayattu martial arts. I don't think I had been this excited since my wedding day; I was so ready to find peace again. When I got off the plane, a bus was waiting for me and everyone else who was heading to the center. I quickly jumped on and excitedly talked to everyone on the bus, most of whom could not understand a word I was saying. I found a small group of Americans and made my way over to them. Many of them were coming just to relax from their hectic lives. Some were coming because they had come before. But a few, like myself, were coming to find out more about themselves—to understand the heartbreak they had gone through in life and to find who they truly were. Those were the people I was interested in getting to know.

"When we got off the bus, a small Indian man greeted us. He was a very happy man, and something about him just spilled out joy and contentment. I couldn't help but feel jealous of this man; he just seemed so alive. If anyone knew what it meant to 'rage against the dying of the light,' it was this man.

"'Namaste, everyone,' the man said with a heavy accent and broken English, bowing to the group. 'I would like to welcome to India and thank you for coming. During your time here, we will be getting very close to one another, and I hope to know who you really are by the end of this journey. Let me start by introducing myself. My name is Vivek, which in English means "discerning wisdom." Which means you can't hide anything from me ... just kidding. I will be your guide through your classes and will be sharing a lot about myself in the near future.'"

"Wait a second," Jordan interrupted. "The little Indian dude's name was Vivek, and you just stole it because you liked it?"

Vivek laughed. "Jordan, just be quiet and listen. I didn't steal anyone's name; it was given to me. My time in India was one of the greatest times of my life, besides my time with Emma. At that center, there were no expectations of what a man should be like, like there are in America. I wasn't given some false sense of identity like the media and churches often do here. I was free to learn who I was on my own. 'Discerning Wisdom' was the greatest name for that man.

"After Vivek, our guide, had taken us to our rooms, we were instructed to meet in the dining hall. When I got there, I saw a massive spread of amazing food set out before us. It was all vegetarian food—I must have missed that on the website—but it still looked amazing. I remember sitting there for hours, eating with the staff and all the students that night. We were all complete strangers, yet it felt like a family reunion. I miss those dinners, I really do.

"After a while, Vivek came up to me and whispered in my ear, 'May I speak with you, sir?'

"I got up and followed Vivek into the hall.

"'Your name Saul Treeborn, correct?' he asked me.

"'Yes, it is, sir,' I answered.

"'I need to know why you are here, Saul. I need to know what brought you to this center.'

"'I came to find my name, sir,' I replied timidly.

"'But your name Saul Treeborn, I thought. What are you looking for?' the man asked, almost with a humorous tone.

"I had no idea what to say. 'I ... uh ... I don't know how to explain what I mean, sir. I am looking to find out who I really am,' I said.

"Vivek looked at me for a second and then busted out laughing. 'Ha-ha-ha-ha, Saul, you looked so scared. What you think I do? Kick you out? No. I will tell you this, Saul. At the end of three months, I give you new name. Sound good, huh? Brand-spanking-new. I already have one in mind,' Vivek said in broken English, then he slapped me on the cheek and walked away, laughing. Everyone had failed to mention that he was kind of a jokester. But there was still something so sweet about this man. I knew I needed to know him more.

"Over the course of the next few months, I found out more about myself than I ever thought I was going to. I tackled the wounds from my father. I came to grips with my actions that had led to Emma's death, and I finally forgave myself for the mistakes I had made. I grew so much. I even started to help some of the other students with the trauma they were facing. I felt free again. And I learned Kalaripayattu, which I will have to admit, I was never really good at. But if I needed to impress a child with my moves, I probably could. For the first time since I got out of rehab, I felt free. I needed rehab—it got me to a place where I could do something like this, like going to India. When I got out of rehab, though, I wasn't free. I was fighting to keep my head above water and not drown from my addiction again. That poem I told you about did not free me; it just put things into perspective. Understanding that life is short, that there is a 'dying of the light,' makes life more precious and me anxious to live. But here ... here I became free.

"Every night at dinner, Vivek would walk over to me and whisper in my ear, 'May I speak with you, sir?' He would pull me aside and ask me the same question he did the first night. 'Your name Saul Treeborn, correct?'

"'Yes, it is, sir,' I always answered, hoping for

something new from him.

"'I need to know why you are here, Saul. I need to know what brought you to this center,' he would say.

"I would always respond, 'I am looking for my name.'

"Vivek would always bust out laughing, just as he did the first night, and say, 'I thought your name was Saul. Every night you crack me up, Saul. Every night.' He would always say something to that effect, slap me on the cheek, and then walk away. Never anything more and never anything less. I was convinced this man was out of his mind!

"Finally, one night I asked him, 'Why do you ask me the same question every night and then just laugh at the answer?'

"Vivek scratched his chin. 'I don't know why I ask you same question, Saul. I only know why I laugh. You come here searching for name, yes?'

"'Yeah, that is what I have told you every single night,' I answered, slightly frustrated.

"'So you come looking for name when you already have one. That funny, Saul. It is like monkey climbing a big, tall tree, looking for a banana, when he has a whole bundle of bananas sitting at the bottom of a tree. It funny.' Vivek couldn't stop himself from laughing some more.

"'Vivek, I don't get what you mean, honestly,' I said.

"He stopped laughing immediately, looked at me, and said, 'Saul, you struggle with what your father did to you. You struggle with what you did to your wife. And all the while you struggle, you find the time to help others here at the center. You are needy, but when you see a need, you fill it. When I said you already have a name, I didn't mean *Saul*—I meant you have already found your name. Yet you are still climbing the tree looking for a banana.' Then he patted my cheek and walked away.

"I walked back to my room with a head full of thoughts and began to meditate as we had been taught. We only had about a week left at the center, and Vivek never pulled me aside again. In fact, he rarely even said hi. I focused on his words from that night, hoping to understand, but never got it. I hoped that Vivek would pull me aside and explain, but he never did. So I just focused on my meditation and tried to learn as much as possible in the time that was left. On my last night, I packed my bags and prepared to leave. As I began to meditate, a note slid under my door that said, *Hey, monkey! Stop climbing for bananas and just enjoy them already. You good man, Saul, but not very smart.* I laughed because I could hear Vivek's broken English speaking in this letter. I didn't know what he meant, but I lay down with a huge grin on my face. I had peace, and if that was all I walked away with, then that was enough for me.

"I got up the next morning, got my bags on the bus, and looked around for Vivek, but he was nowhere to be found. I told one of the staff to tell Vivek I would miss him. I got on the bus to the airport, where I would then head to Israel. When we got to the airport, Vivek was standing outside the bus, holding a sign that said, 'Nice to meet you, Discerning Wisdom.' I walked up to him, and we both embraced for a final good-bye. I asked him what his sign meant, and he said, 'I promised you a new name, Saul, and this is it.'

"'I am sorry, Vivek, but I don't understand,' I said. 'This is your name in English.'

"Vivek smiled at me. 'I know it is. That is what we have in common, Saul. We look at a hurting soul and we discern what is needed. We are discerning wisdom. We put our pain aside for the betterment of others. I know you were selfish in the past, but so was I, and that doesn't define who you are now. You good man. Stop climbing the trees looking for bananas, you stupid monkey. Enjoy helping others. It was nice getting to know you, Vivek.'

"This once complete stranger came into my life and gave me a name. I set out to rage against death, and in that I found life. I wiped the tears from my eyes and hugged Vivek good-bye. I boarded the plane with a new name, and in that moment, I knew who I was."

Chapter 17
The Tamarisk Tree

Vivek sat across the fire, looking up at the sky with the biggest grin on his face. It was the first time since he'd started his story tonight that he seemed to be happy and seemed to have a sense of peace about him. It was clear that India had a lasting impact on him. I couldn't help but understand his joy during that time of his life. He'd been looking for answers, and a complete stranger had given him those answers. Even gave him a new name, but also spoke purpose into that new name in a way that taught him how to live again.

In contrast, I started to understand the man Vivek thought I was. Ezra had been my name since birth, yet the name Vivek described for me was something much different, something new and something powerful. Something I did not understand. If I could grasp that identity for myself, if I could own the name for myself, I could see how life would take on new meaning and purpose much like Vivek's had. Despite all the anxiety and confusion this new name brought, I felt joy. *Ezra* was becoming something so much more powerful than ever before. I didn't understand what was happening, but I knew there was joy inside of me.

"So, what happened to your teacher Indian Vivek?" Daniel asked.

"I don't know. I haven't seen him since that day. I loved that man. One day I hope to go see him again, but I am sure he is calling some American a monkey and slapping them as he walks away," Vivek said. He touched his cheek and smiled to himself.

"So, what happened in Israel then?" I asked him, excited to understand how his journey could speak more to this identity I was starting to understand for myself.

"Well, Ezra, that is actually where I met Connor. Life showed me my new name and intended me to start using it as soon as possible."

"What do you mean?" I asked.

"Well, I had been in Israel for about a month, just sightseeing mostly and meeting the locals. Unlike when I was India, I didn't have a set agenda during my trip to Israel. I chose to travel to Israel because there is an almost mythical atmosphere to it. So much of the world's history has been defined by what happened there. It is also the epicenter for some of the most profound spiritual awakenings and spiritual movements in history like Judaism, Christianity, and Islam. So, being a history teacher, I couldn't help myself. More importantly, though, I thought if I was going to find a deeper meaning to life, a 'grand design' to everything I had been through, I thought Israel would be the place. So I went with no agenda, just sightseeing and trusting that what needed to happen would.

"My goal was to go and eat with a new family every week and see what I could learn from them. Unfortunately, though, I wasn't able to make friends as quickly as I'd expected, but I was able to share a meal with a few families every month. It was beautiful spending time with locals and listening to people's stories. I heard stories of religion like I have never heard before. Muslims spoke about the Quran with a beautiful passion. Jewish families were still living out the Old Testament in the Holy Land. I heard marvelous stories that I had never heard before. It was just an amazing time in Israel, meeting people and enjoying the history. For a history nerd like myself, it was the greatest thing I could ask for.

"One day I was out hiking, and I saw a good-sized group of Americans surrounding a tree. It struck me as odd because I hadn't really seen any Americans for a while, and yet here was a group of about ten of them standing around some random tree. A man was standing in front of the tree, talking about something. I remember thinking that the man talked with his hands a lot because I could see him from the hill that I was hiking on."

Jordan stopped Vivek there. "We already know you are talking about Connor. That guy talks with his hands way too much." We all shared in the laughter.

Vivek continued. "I walked down to join them and hear what the man was saying. As I got closer, the gentleman yelled out, 'Come join us, brother. We are just talking about this tree here.' I stood behind a few people, close enough so I could hear him.

"'This, ladies and gentlemen, is a tamarisk tree or, as it's often called, a salt cedar. This is the same type of tree that Abraham from the Bible planted in the land of Beersheba. Does anyone notice anything about this tree that is different than some of the other ones we have seen?'

"A woman raised her hand and said, 'It looks like it might be bigger than the rest.'

"Then a man raised his hand and said, 'It gives a large amount of shade.'

"The man standing in front of the tree got very excited about that last comment and said, 'Yes! What else about the shade?'

"I raised my hand and said, 'The shade seems cooler than the shade from other trees. I have been here for about a month, and I've noticed it seems much cooler under these tam ... a ... r ... what trees? I'm sorry. I don't remember the name.'

"The man smiled and nodded his head in agreement. 'Exactly, exactly right, Mr. ...?'

"'Vivek,' I replied.

"'Beautiful name, Mr. Vivek. You're very right; the shade of this tree is cooler than some of the other trees in the desert because of the salt. You see, at night the salt in these pine needles soaks up the moisture in the air. In the morning, you can actually see drops of water dripping down the tree. Now in the daytime, the water slowly evaporates, creating a cooler shade. If you are wandering in the desert, this is the kind of tree that you really want to find. It provides the biggest and coolest shade and can be used in a lot of different ways. Some of the other benefits of this tree are that you can take these pine needles and make tea. You can take the sap from this tree and make medicine. The wood from this tree is also extremely strong and hard to break. This is the Swiss Army knife of desert trees. The only other thing to keep in mind about this tree is that it takes an extremely long time to grow. If you planted this tree in the ground, it would take almost one hundred years before it reached the height of a child. So, why would anyone plant this tree in their backyard?'

"Everyone was silent. No one knew the answer.

"'I'll tell you,' the man said. 'The tamarisk tree is a statement. Whenever new land was obtained, the Jewish community would plant one of these trees as a symbol for the future generations. This isn't a tree that you plant for your benefit or pleasure. No one would plant a tamarisk tree to enjoy the pleasure of its cool shade and tea. This tree takes so long to grow that you would die long before you would ever reap the benefits. No, this tree is planted for your children and your children's children. You plant this tree because you want your grandkids to be able to relax in the cool breeze. You do this because you want to leave your grandchildren something that will give them comfort in the desert. The Jewish people knew they would not be able to enjoy the benefits of this tree, but they planted it as a symbol of their commitment to their family and loved ones.'

"The man continued talking some more about the tree as I started to walk away. It seemed silly at the time, but oddly enough, the idea of the tamarisk tree resonated with me. The Jewish people wanted their children to know that the previous generations were committed to their care and comfort. They wanted their grandchildren to enjoy the coolness of the day. They wanted their offspring to never go through the desert without the shade of a tamarisk tree. I found a rock away from the group and sat down to think about it all. I had been through so much pain and suffering in my life. I had struggled through so much depression and anger that most men will never know. I had seen things in this world that would make others sick to think about. Yet I sat there so far away from home with complete joy and at complete peace with it all. This pain and suffering led me to a place where I could truly be free. So the question was, How do I plant a tamarisk tree for future children and their children? How do I give them the shade in the desert I never had? My pain couldn't be in vain.

"As I pondered these things, I heard someone walking toward me. It was the man who had been speaking by the tree earlier.

"'Vivek, right?' he said, sitting down next to me. 'Nice to meet you, Vivek. My name is Connor. I am a counselor in Las Vegas, Nevada. Ever been there?'

"'No, I have never been there. I am from New York though. Born and raised,' I replied.

"'I had a feeling you were from the States. That is such an interesting name, Vivek. What is it?' he asked.

"'Well, my real name is Saul Treeborn,' I said, 'but I have been on a search for who I am for a little while now. I just left India about a month back, and the name Vivek was given to me.'

"'What does it mean?' he asked.

"I told him that it meant 'discerning wisdom.' Then Connor and I spoke for a while about some of the things that had led up to this moment in my life. I told him about my addictions and rehab, and I even told him about the poem, but I didn't mention Emma. Seeing he was a counselor who clearly had some religious ties, I figured he would shun me based on everything I told him, but he just kept pushing for more and more. He really seemed to care. For some reason, this random stranger felt like a best friend to me. He invited me to have dinner with him that night, and I accepted his offer. We shook hands, planned to meet up later, and went our separate ways.

"As I continued my hike, I thought about everything Connor and I had talked about. I also thought about the tamarisk tree and how that fit into my story. I couldn't help but feel like this day was meant to be and that Connor and I were supposed to meet. We had dinner that night, and our friendship continued to grow over the course of the next two months. An hour or two before I had to head back home, I met with Connor for lunch and asked him, 'When are you and your group headed back to Vegas?'

"He laughed a little. 'Vivek, my group left a month ago. I stayed behind.'

"'Why did you stay behind?' I asked.

"'I stayed behind to get to know you.'

"At that point, I really didn't understand why a complete stranger would stay in a foreign country to get to know me. I was nothing special.

"'Why did you stay back to get to know me?' I laughed awkwardly.

"'After we had dinner together that day I first met you, something insane happened. When I went to bed, I had the strangest dream about a woman. She told me that I needed to get to know you more and that I needed to stay. The next morning, I called my office and canceled my upcoming appointments. I figured, I hadn't taken a vacation in years, so what could be the harm in seeing where things went? The following night I had another dream, and this time you and the woman were sitting together, holding hands and looking at one another under that tamarisk tree where we first met. I walked up to you two, and you turned your head and just simply stated, "Help me plant my tamarisk tree." Since then, I have been racking my brain trying to figure out what that might mean, and then it hit me. I have been trying to start a young men's mentorship program in Vegas for a long time. The whole idea behind it is helping young men get a grasp on their identity and discover who they are, which is what your entire journey has been about. I see such amazing potential in you, Vivek. You are exactly the kind of man I have been looking for. I know it sounds weird. I am sure the dream was just too much ice cream before bed, but it doesn't change the fact that you are the man for the job. So I stayed to offer you a job in Vegas, Vivek. Will you come plant your tamarisk tree?'

"I had no idea what to say. I had never been to the West Coast. There I was, sitting in Israel, and this man I had only known for two months wanted me to come work for him in Las Vegas. Every bone in my body was telling me that I should say no, that I should get on a plane, go back home, and never look back. I knew I didn't have a job waiting for me, but I knew it wouldn't take long to find one. New York was all I had ever known. It was safe and familiar territory. But that poem kept running through my head. The answer just came out of me: 'Okay, Connor, when do I start?'

"We both started laughing and talking about the craziness of the situation. We talked about how it just seemed that everything had lined up for this to happen to me. If one tiny piece of the puzzle was missing, I never would have come to Vegas, and I never would have met you fine young gentlemen. Connor drove me to the airport. We both shook hands, and I started to walk away. Then something struck me: Who was the woman in the dreams?

"'Connor, what was the woman's name in your dream? Did she tell you?' I asked.

"'She never told me. Why?' he asked.

"I pulled out my wallet and grabbed a picture of Emma and held it in my hand. Connor stood there, waiting for me to say something, but I just smiled and placed the photo back in my pocket. I wanted the woman in his dream to be Emma. I wanted her to still be watching out for me, loving me from her next life. In that moment, I chose to believe that Emma was guiding my future. Helping me break the cycle of pain in my life.

"'Why are you crying, Vivek?' Connor asked, with a large smile. He probably assumed they were tears of joy from the job offer.

"'I love my wife. I miss my wife,' I replied.

"Connor looked confused. 'You never mentioned you were married. I am truly sorry if that complicates things.'

"'No, no, don't apologize. She passed away a while back. I just wish she could see the man I have become,' I replied, smiling.

"I spent the next hour telling him about Emma and how that played into my story. I had left all that out before because I thought Connor would judge me, given the fact that I had cheated on her and that she had committed suicide after she found out. Connor never explicitly said he was religious, but it was clear. However, he never skipped a beat. He listened intently and just embraced me at the end when he saw the pain in my eyes.

"It was time to go. Tears ran down my face as I boarded the plane. People must have thought I was losing my mind, but oddly enough, I was just full of joy. I believed Emma still loved me after everything I had done to her. I have no reason to believe the woman in

Connor's dream was Emma, but I do. I want it to be her. It has to be her. Emma still loves me. I found my name, and Emma helped me find my purpose in this world. I was going to Vegas to plant my tamarisk tree."

Chapter 18
I Fight to Break the Cycle

"So we are your tamarisk tree?" I asked Vivek.

"Yes, Ezra, you boys are why I moved from New York to here," Vivek stated proudly.

"So why tell us all of this? Why not just tell us what our names mean and move on?"

"The Civil War story was what started the process of healing for me. It provided a way of looking at my story and placing it in a context that explained what was truly taking place in my heart and mind—what started my journey to finding who I am and what my name is. It helped me realize that I wasn't fighting the wounds from my father all this time, but I really was fighting myself. My battle was against me. It taught me to take ownership of my life, the good and the bad, and break the cycle of hurt in my family. The poem pushed me to seek out who I am and not just give in to my situation. It showed me I needed to learn to live. India helped me find my name, and Israel helped me find my purpose. All of that was great, but this ... this right here, all of us sitting here, is what it was all leading to. If one thing was different, if one thing was changed—if I didn't go to India or if I didn't go on that hike in Israel—we would not be sitting here, going through all of this together. I didn't just sit you down and tell you your names because, if I did, it wouldn't mean anything. I needed you to struggle with me and hear the pain that led to this point. I needed you to understand the power of a story. I needed you to see the work that went into this very moment and for you to see the importance of the journey you are starting in your life. You needed to hear my story before you could understand my name. Growing a tamarisk tree is a lot of work, and it takes time. You, gentlemen, are my tamarisk tree."

I didn't know exactly how I felt being compared to a tree. Yes, Vivek's story was insane, and who could honestly listen to that story and not feel something for the guy? But really, all of this, for me? For Jordan and Daniel? He went through all of this pain and here he was retelling everything to us to just ... plant a tree? It didn't make any sense to me. I really didn't feel that important. Vivek had lost his wife, gone to rehab, and traveled the world looking for his meaning in life, and here he was saying that his meaning in life was to reach out to me. Yeah, I was sure I would do some cool stuff in my life but nothing worth the pain Vivek had gone through. All of this made me feel guilty. He took us out here to become men and to discover ourselves, but something wasn't clicking for me.

"Ezra, you look distracted. You okay?" Vivek asked.

"I can't help but feel like you wasted your time on us, or at least on me," I responded, putting my head down in shame.

"Why would you say that?" he asked.

"Because you went through so much to get to this point, and it just doesn't seem worth it. I mean, yeah, I get excited, like any boy would, when you talk about my name and call me 'powerful.' I mean, who wouldn't? But I am not some bird of prey, Vivek; I am not some mighty warrior who was born to lead armies to battle. I am not who you think I am. I mean, my dad doesn't even see me as a real man. He is always making fun of my hair or how I dress and calling me gay, like I am some soft version of the son he wanted to have. I'm just not the guy you say I am. I am just a fourteen-year-old boy trying to conquer video games and school. You wasted your time, Vivek." I was crying as I said all of this. The most upsetting part for me was that this weak identity felt so much more real than the identity Vivek had given me. Everything he had said about me felt so close, like it could be real, but it felt just out of my grasp. I didn't know what it took to become a man, but it didn't feel like I had it. I felt like a little child who was playing Cowboys and Indians. It was all an act, just another a game.

"Ezra, let me ask you something. How did we get here? On top of this rock tonight, how did we get here?" Vivek asked.

I tried to figure out the point Vivek was trying to

make, but I couldn't see where he was going with this. "We hiked, I guess," I finally answered.

"Well, yes, I guess you could say we hiked, but there was more than that. How did we get on top of this rock?" he asked, probing for the right answer.

"I don't know, man. We climbed a ladder after walking through a canyon for a long time," I replied.

Vivek continued, "All of that is technically true, Ezra, but that isn't the answer I am looking for. That isn't how we got to the top of this rock. Besides how we physically got here, how else did we get here? I know that sounds confusing, but just try and think about it."

Vivek had lost me at this point. How do you get somewhere other than physically? I pondered the question for what felt like a while. I tried to think about what he asked in an abstract meaning but still could not think of what he meant.

Vivek saw the confusion on my face. "I know that question didn't make a lot sense, but do you have a guess for what I am trying to get at?"

"I honestly have no idea what you are talking about, Vivek," I said.

"I had a feeling that question wouldn't make a lot of sense," he said, laughing to himself. "We struggled, Ezra. That is how we got on top of this rock. The hike and the climb were just the external displays of our struggle, but inside we struggled with a lot more than just some hike. Are you starting to see what I am getting at?" he asked.

I shook my head no.

"You said not too long ago that you don't feel like a

man and that you think you wasted my time," Vivek said. "You said that you are weak and that you don't feel powerful like I believe you are. That is because you are struggling, Ezra. I watched all three of you as I told you we needed to get on top of this rock. I heard you complain and groan about how there was no way to the top. Some of you cried. I listened to your fears and worries about being lost while we walked through the canyon. You struggled to get to this place, to the top of this rock. Your identity isn't something that is just handed to you by some guy sitting around a fire, talking about his life. It isn't something that can just be lightly grasped, and it isn't something that will ever come easy. Your identity, who you truly are, is a struggle and always will be. I know who you are, Ezra. I can see it in the way you look at life. Your name means 'mighty helper,' and I can see that is true. You are not what others say you are. You are strong and courageous. You are truly like a bird of prey. But I also know that the person I see sitting in front me hasn't accepted it yet, and that's okay. None of you have truly struggled with your identity yet. It took time and effort to get to the top of this rock. It took tears and a lot of pain, but guess what? We have been sitting at the top of this rock for a few hours now. Finding your identity as a man will take a lot of effort. It will take tears and pain, but if you stay the course, if you find your way through the canyon and climb the ladder that leads to who you really are, you will find yourself sitting at the top. You will see who you are and see your identity with a clear view. You will see clearly all the beauty and pain that led to this point. You will see all the mountains and valleys, and the path home will be clear. You will have struggled and made it out in the end."

It wasn't that everything Vivek just said finally clicked with me and I knew who I was. It wasn't that I felt better about Vivek putting so much energy and time into me. I just knew that Vivek was right. I could sit there and listen all day about how powerful of a man I was. I could have a thousand people tell me who I was and what my name meant, but it wouldn't change a thing. Because I hadn't struggled with my identity for a long time. The problem became so clear. My generation wanted everything right now, instant gratification. This trip wasn't just about giving us new names; it was about starting a lifelong process of finding our identities. What finally clicked for me in that moment wasn't some new form of identity but a realization that Saul Treeborn ... was always Vivek. It wasn't until Saul fought against himself that he learned his identity.

My dad was not to blame for the way I felt about myself. I could choose to accept the way I was or not, but there was no one to blame but me. I had let the views of others become my identity. I had taken the actions of my enemies and turned them into a mask, which I wore as my identity. As it turned out, the enemy was me all along. I was the reason I felt weak. I was the reason I was scared to lead. It wasn't my father's fault or the bullies' or anyone else's; it was mine. In that moment, I knew I needed to struggle if I ever wanted to know how powerful I could really be.

Seeing the wheels turning inside my head, Vivek called for my attention. "Ezra."

"Yes?" I responded.

"Earlier I asked you a question. It was a simple question, but I want you to think and answer it again. After everything you have heard tonight and after everything that I have said about you, I want you to rethink your answer. Why do you fight, Ezra?"

I chuckled to myself, seeing that this was the exact discussion I was having with myself.

"I fight to break the cycle."

Vivek seemed very interested in my answer. "Can you explain?"

"It wasn't until you decided to fight while you were in rehab that things started to change and you started to make progress. That changed everything. It was not something that you decided to do immediately, but when you did finally fight, you finally understood that the enemy was yourself the whole time. After you got out of rehab, it wasn't until you decided to fight against complacency that you understood life had more to offer. What I mean when I say 'I fight to break the cycle' is that I will never be the man you say I am until I take ownership of my actions and I break the cycle of pain and suffering. I will never face my enemy if I am caught running in a circle."

Daniel and Jordan looked at me like I had just switched places with Vivek.

"Well, I guess you learned something," Jordan said, laughing.

Daniel nodded in agreement. "I like it, man. I like it."

But Vivek stared at me with the look of a proud father. You finally understand, he was probably thinking.

It was funny too, but just by struggling with my own thoughts, I felt closer to the "name" that Vivek had given me. I couldn't say I felt like a man in that moment, but I sure felt a lot closer to being one. I was learning to fight.

"You are a good man, Ezra Joel Matthews. I think I planted my tree in the right place. You are all great men, and I can't wait to help you gentlemen find your way in this next season. Facing yourself on the battlefield is never easy, but neither was getting on top of this rock. We must fight. Always remember the poem that I read to you," Vivek said, then held his fist in the air. "I think we have done enough talking for one night," he continued. "Let's get some rest so we are ready for the hike down the rock tomorrow. Sleep tight, men."

Chapter 19
The Calling

That night I had the same dream I'd had the night before I came on this trip. A war was at hand. I dreamed of a great battle, but something was different this time. I was standing in the desert, in the heat of day, in front of a vast army of a thousand men. Evil was written on the hearts of these men. I looked all around and didn't see any green grass nor any ponds or rivers or anything of beauty. Just as before, I was alone in the Valley of Fire. I was scared once again, terrified of what was to come. But not hopeless, not this time. I looked around again and started to see meaning and wonder. In the midst of chaos and fury, I saw peace and truth. Unlike the first time I had this dream, I saw hope. Surrounded by nothing but hungry men aching for a battle, I stood with confidence, not because fear was absent but because fear led to my strength. Questions of doubt left my mind; instead, curiosity took its place. Who are these men? Where are they from? Why are they fighting? Questions filled my mind but did not calm my fear. My heart was beating so fast that I swore I must have been surrounded by the beating of war drums ... and then it happened. The vast army started their descent down the dirt-covered hill toward me. All I could see was this massive black wave moving toward me through a great cloud of dust and rubble. This time I did not look for somewhere to hide, because I knew in that moment that I must fight. I took a symbolic step forward, clearing my mind of distractions. I grabbed a handful of dirt and let it fall between my fingers. I began to count the seconds as my enemy moved closer and closer. Five. Four. I took my stance and broadened my shoulders. Three. I drew my sword. Two. One. I spit on the ground and braced myself for battle. Zero. I swung away at my enemy with eyes wide-open, gripping my sword with white knuckles. Before, fear had prevented me from opening my eyes and seeing the face of my enemy, but this time I fought proudly, making eye contact with every swing of my sword. And you know what I saw? I saw the vast army was myself. Every single one of these men was me. So I stood and fought, struggling through the chaos. And when I did so ... I woke up.

The dream felt so real, just as before, but this time I woke up with pride, knowing that I was beginning to face my biggest enemy: myself. When I woke up, everyone was already awake, cooking bacon and eggs over the fire.

"You all right, Ezra? Sounded like you were having a bad dream or something," Jordan asked.

I smiled. "Yeah, I'm good, man, thanks."

I didn't need to tell them about my dream because it was for me. I had begun the same journey that Vivek had, and that wasn't for anyone other than myself. I wasn't learning how to find my name for my parents or to look cool for my friends. I wasn't doing it for Vivek or for anyone else. This was for me.

"Want some breakfast, man, or are you going to sit over there looking pretty all day?" Jordan grinned at me.

I laughed and walked over to grab some bacon. "Thanks, man," I said around a mouthful.

The three of us sat there talking about what the future might hold for us. Daniel talked about how he realized he didn't want to be some football superstar anymore, but he wanted to become a counselor just like Connor and help kids going through growing up with only one parent. Jordan talked about how he wanted to teach in a university one day, maybe history. He said that it was clear how to prepare for the future by looking backward and that he wished his parents had done a better job of preparing for the future.

"What about you, Ezra? What do you think you will be doing in life?" Daniel asked.

I didn't know what I wanted. I couldn't tell them my future goals because I didn't have any yet. So I told them the truth.

"I don't know, man. I guess wherever I end up is where I should be. All I know is I want to be everything Vivek said about me, and I am going to spend my time figuring that out."

Jordan and Daniel nodded. I looked over at Vivek,

who was tending to the fire. He had the same look of pride on his face as he had the night before. I guess he knew that he had successfully planted a seed in each of us. The tamarisk tree was growing.

"You guys ready to head back down to the van? We gotta head home today," Vivek said.

"Yeah, I think we are all ready," I replied on behalf of the group.

We spent the next ten minutes or so cleaning up and then started walking. We got to the ladder and climbed back into the canyon. When we got back down, we hiked the same as we did before, which took a couple of hours, but we all had a strong sense of confidence this time. There were no more tears or complaining. We were men on a mission.

"You see, men, struggle leads to confidence. This was not an easy hike yesterday for you guys, and now you all look like you are on your way to a fire. Struggle makes a man," Vivek said to us as we hiked.

"Yeah, yeah, we get it," Jordan responded, laughing. But it was true. The struggle we had faced the day before gave us confidence for today.

We finally reached the hole in the rock, we all got on our hands and knees and crawled through. Vivek was the first one through, so he stood on the other side and gave each of us a hand. When we were all out, we shook the sand off our clothes and started walking to the van.

We saw a group of men standing around the van, and as we got closer, we noticed that they were my dad, Jordan's dad, also Connor. We were so excited to see them. We ran to them and gave them each a huge hug. We had a few minutes to talk and hang out. Daniel looked sad that his father wasn't there. Vivek talked with him while Jordan and I told our fathers all about our weekend.

Then Vivek gave us some instructions. "Gentlemen, if I can get your attention for a second. Connor has supplied all of us with some lunch, so we are going to eat and spend some time together. Then I am going to lead us all to a small spot before we head home. There the fathers have something that they want to do with you boys, so I hope you weren't planning on leaving yet."

We had no idea what this meant, but we were very excited.

Chapter 20
Nice to Meet You, Mr. Matthews

After we spent some time together, we left the site and drove for about an hour in the direction of home. It was getting close to sunset, and I was beginning to think Vivek had forgotten about going anywhere else. We passed the time talking about the stories Vivek had told us, some of which shocked our fathers. All of a sudden, Vivek drove off the side of the road and said, "We are here, gentlemen."

We all got out of the van, and Connor lit a torch to lead the way. About a quarter of a mile later, we reached a natural amphitheater made by the surrounding rocks, and in the center, we saw a mountain of wooden pallets and trash. In front of the pile of wood was a sword stuck into the ground. The smell of lighter fluid filled the air. Connor was smiling, and it was clear this was his favorite part. It was kind of creepy at first. Vivek walked over and hugged him.

"Gentlemen, come stand over here in front of me,"

Connor said. "We read about 'coming of age' rituals throughout history where leaders call the man out of boys. That is why we are here. The past few days Vivek has been challenging the way you see the struggles in your life. He has been challenging you to think about who you really are and how you see yourself. But your fathers and I have come here to call you into manhood. From this point forward, you are a man. You will leave childish things here and live in the identity of a man. That does not mean you have to go out and get a job and live by yourself now. But it does mean you are responsible for your life and for your actions from this point forward. Fathers, can I have you come and stand next to me?" Connor waited until they were standing next to each other, and then he turned his back to us. He threw the torch into the mountain of wood, and it lit up like a Christmas tree. The flames reached so high that it filled the amphitheater with light.

Connor turned back around and drew the sword out of the ground. "Daniel, please take a step forward and kneel," he instructed.

Daniel walked up to Connor and got onto one knee.

Connor took the sword and placed the blade on Daniel's shoulder. "You are Daniel. Your name means 'God is my judge.' Historically, Daniel was a great Jewish prophet who lived during the time of exile for the Israelites. He became powerful in the kingdom of Babylon by interpreting dreams. He also spent time in a den of lions and slept among them without harm. Daniel was a man of courage. He stood in front of the king and gave him interpretations of his dreams, many of which should have gotten him killed. He slept in a den of lions that should have taken his life. Yet he did so boldly. You are courage. You are a man of great wisdom. But most importantly, you answer to God alone. Daniel, live in the knowledge that you were meant to walk this earth with courage and wisdom written on your heart." Connor paused, taking a knee and wiping a tear from Daniel's eyes. He placed his hand on the side of Daniel's head while making eye contact with him.

Connor continued softly, "Your father may not be here to witness this moment, but we are. We will always be there for you, no matter what. We will always encourage you and push you to be the man you are meant to be. Daniel, never forget: Love compassionately. Fight honorably. Learn continuously. And live with the knowledge that you are loved. Daniel, welcome to manhood." Connor took the sword and moved it to the other shoulder. They both stood up and hugged, after which the sword was handed to Jordan's father.

"Jordan, please take a step forward and kneel." His father placed the blade on Jordan's shoulder. "You are Jordan. Your name means 'to flow down.' Your name is at the center of a lot of great historical events. During the time of the Crusades, men would bring water from the Jordan to baptize their children, and the name became popular in England because of it. Do you understand what that says about you, son? You are a mighty force. When you live in the truth of your identity, people will flock to you. The Jordan River is a strong, powerful force, yet it holds mystery and beauty with every drop. People come from all around the world to see this mighty river. Son, you were born to be a mighty force in the world. You were born to share your strength with everyone you meet just like the people who brought water from the Jordan to their children. You have told me that you wish to be a teacher. Live in the knowledge of your name because, if you do, your strength and power will always flow down to those you teach."

It was such a beautiful sight to see Jordan's father speak those words over his son. With this mighty fire behind them and the blade on his shoulder, I couldn't help but be brought to tears. In the wrong hands, a sword could be deadly and bring great tragedy, but in the right hands, like those of Jordan's father, it can bring the power of a man out of a boy.

"Son, love compassionately. Fight honorably. Learn continuously. And live with the knowledge that you are loved. Jordan, welcome to manhood." His father took the sword and moved it to the other shoulder. Jordan stood up, and he and his father embraced passionately and wept with joy in sharing this moment.

Now it was my turn. My heart was pounding with nervousness. Why? It wasn't that big of a deal. Yet something inside of me knew it was. Something inside of me knew that this was the day everything would change, but was I ready? My heart continued to pound, and just like in my dream, it started to sound like war drums. I watched as Jordan's father handed the sword to my father.

"Ezra, please take a step forward and kneel," my father said.

I walked up to my father and took a knee while he placed the sword on my shoulder. I looked up at my father, and he had the biggest grin on his face, a profound look of such intensity that I had never seen before. He was so proud of me, and I didn't know why, but that smile made me feel like more of a man than anything Vivek had to say. A single tear fell down his cheek, followed by a crackle in his voice as he started to speak.

"Your name is Ezra. Your name means 'powerful helper.' In Jewish history, after the exile of Israel, the temple was no more. After some time in Babylon, the king released the Jews to go back and rebuild their temple. There were plenty of people working on the temple, but Ezra went back to work on their hearts. He stirred the hearts of the people with passion and power. He didn't do it for fame or power, but he did it because his love was so rich and plentiful that he needed to share it. Ezra, you are power. The verb used with your name literally refers to a bird of prey. Your name is everything that I hope to be as a father, as a husband, as a man. You are a mighty helper. You are a warrior who helps his brother in combat, not out of duty but because he loves them. You stir the hearts of everyone you touch with compassion and fury; you stir my heart, son. You are a beautiful bird of prey. Live in the knowledge that you were born on this earth to help others by stirring up their hearts with power and love. Never forget who you are, and never stop fighting to be more. You are not weak, son. You are so strong."

My dad bent down on one knee and brought his head near mine. Then he whispered so that only I could hear, "I can see how much you are hurting, son. I can see that you think you are ugly, that you are ashamed of who you are in the mirror. I am so sorry if I ever did anything to make you feel that way. You are the most beautiful child I could have ever asked for. Never walk a day on this earth without knowing how much I love you, Ezra." He wiped the tears from his face and stood back up.

The tears seemed to pour out of me. For the first time in my life, I knew I was becoming a man. I wasn't naïve; I knew that there was going to be a lot of work and struggle ahead. My father's words were clear—this was going to be a lifelong process. Saying some words with a sword didn't give my father the power to take all the trials and pain away. But he didn't need to. In that moment, my father changed my life.

My father placed his hand under my chin, lifting my face so I could see him. He picked up some dirt and mixed it with my tears. He then took his thumb, dipped it in the wet dirt, and placed it on the middle of my forehead, leaving a thumbprint of mud made by my tears. He whispered in my ear, "Son, let this thumbprint be a reminder of this place inside you. Never forget what happened here tonight."

He stood back up and said, "Ezra Joel Matthews. Love compassionately. Fight honorably. Learn continuously. And live with the knowledge that you, my son, are loved. Ezra Joel ... welcome to manhood."

I jumped up, almost knocking the sword out of my father's hand, and wrapped my arms around his neck.

"I love you, son, and I am so proud of you," he said over and over again.

I could see Connor hugging Daniel.

"Your father would be so proud, Daniel, just like I am. You are a great man," Connor was saying to him. I couldn't hear the rest of what he said to Daniel, but I didn't need to. Daniel was weeping with happiness, and so was I.

After all the hugging, crying, and laughing was over, Connor took the sword and thrust it back into the ground.

"Men, never forget this day," he said. "This is the day you chose to fight instead of hide. This is the day you decided to love instead of hate. This is the day you became men. I love all of you, and I am privileged to have served you. I know Vivek wants to say something."

Vivek stepped forward with something in his hand.

"It was my honor to be on this journey with you men. I have learned something about myself from each and every one of you. You are all going to be amazing men, and I am so grateful Connor brought us all together. In my hand I have an envelope for each of you. Inside is a key chain that will serve as a reminder to love compassionately. Fight honorably. Learn continuously. And live with the knowledge that you are loved. The second thing in the envelope is the poem I shared with you last night. I want you to place it somewhere you can see every day and let it remind you of why we are here. I want this poem to be a constant reminder to you of my story and what I went through to get here. Boys fight to be remembered. Men fight to be alive. I hope you all know that I deeply love you and will always be here for you. I enjoyed telling you my story and feel very secure in where I decided to plant my tamarisk tree. Before we go, I want everyone to take that poem out of the envelope, and I want us to read it together."

We all opened our envelopes and unfolded the pieces of paper.

"Read with me," Vivek said.

Facing the fire, we all began to recite the poem. Afterward, we put the flame out and packed up. It was a strange feeling watching as that flame flickered out and died. I thought about the poem as I watched the fire extinguish. You can't expect a flame to keep burning without help, I thought. Even the wildest of fires dies out eventually. But if you struggle, if someone is willing to stir the coals and rekindle the flame, it will never go out. You can't avoid the dying of the light. No one ever can. But if we learn to constantly stir the flame, we will not go gently into that good night.

The car was full of joy and celebration, but I could not stop thinking about that flame. My dad saw that my mind was racing and just put his hand on my shoulder and gave me a grin. I am a man, I kept thinking. And I knew from this day forward nothing would ever be the same.

We finally reached my high school parking lot. The contrast between who we were when we'd been dropped off two days ago and who we were now felt very strange. We had been naïve, childish boys then, and now we held our heads high and our chests forward like men.

My mother was standing there, waiting for us to arrive. My dad walked ahead of me and gave her a kiss on the cheek. When I reached them, he said, "Honey, I want to introduce you to this young man, Mr. Matthews."

I was puzzled as to why my father was introducing me to my mother. But she just smiled, seeing the profound nature of this introduction. In front of her no longer stood her baby boy but a man. Tears streamed down her face as she proudly said, "It sure is nice to meet you, Mr. Matthews."

The End

Afterword

I never had someone like Vivek in my life to take me on a "coming of age" tour and help me navigate the complicated issues we face as we grow up. In middle school, I was beaten up for being overweight, and I struggled with blaming my dad for these issues. I can now say, at twenty-five, I have an amazing relationship with my father, and I feel stupid for thinking that way when I was younger. Through the stories of Saul, Vivek, and Ezra in this book, I have tried to show a profound truth about pain and suffering. We want someone to blame for our suffering. We want to stay ignorant to the causes of our suffering because it seems so much easier. But the more ignorant we are, the more pain we have. This causes a never-ending cycle of suffering. Buddhists have a term for this called *samsara*, which refers to this never-ending cycle of suffering caused by ignorance.

I wrote this book for my son, and my motivation began before he was born. I was working a very boring nine-to-five desk job with plenty of time to reflect on life. I wanted to write something for my son that would explain what I had learned from life. I wanted him to learn from my mistakes, from my story, so that he wouldn't have to repeat them. I also wanted it to have stories, since I always learned best from stories.

Growing up in Las Vegas was difficult. Everything was always about appearance—everyone had to look their best, as if they were ready for a party. Sex, drugs, and gang violence were common at every school I attended. Pornography was available for purchase every couple of blocks—just like newspaper, only fifty cents. Pornography became a major problem for every teenage boy I met in Vegas, myself included.

There were a lot of gray areas to navigate as a teenager in Las Vegas, and the only reason I didn't get lost in it all was because of my family. In writing this book, I wanted my son to feel that support as well. I want him to understand no matter where life takes him, I will always be there for him and support him, even in the darkest of times, just like my parents did for me. So this is my love letter to my son. I never had any intentions on publishing this. In fact, the only reason I sought out an editor was because I am dyslexic and didn't want my son to have to read through all my typos. However, after getting some advice from my fantastic editor at Cypress Editing in Portland, Oregon, she convinced me that this was a valuable lesson that many young men could learn from. So that is what I did.

With this book, I also wanted to convey my love and gratitude to my father. We struggled with many aspects of our relationship when I was growing up. We all make mistakes; we all have faults. I can't tell you how many times he has apologized about calling me gay and making jokes about my appearance now that I am an adult. Being a father myself, I know that I have already said things I wish I could take back. The good my father has done in my life far outweighs any bad. Similar to

Ezra's father in the book, my father never had a dad to look up to. His father tried to kill him and his sisters, abused them, and left their family in financial ruin. My father spent his years traveling from place to place on a motorcycle, trying to figure out all by himself who he was. He has always been there for me and my sister. He has loved us without condition. He spoiled us when he and my mother had the means to do so, which may not have been often, but that just made it so much more special. His love for all of us continues to be unconditional to this day.

Growing up, I hardly ever went to my father (or anyone, honestly) for advice or help. I took care of most issues by myself. I was prideful and arrogant. That is my biggest regret, not taking the time to enjoy the wisdom my father could have given me early on in life, when I could have used it the most—when I needed a Vivek in my life. I am proud that my son will have a grandfather like Neal Frechette to look up to.

Lastly, I want to emphasize the importance of a mother's role in helping young men understand their identity. In the book, Ezra's mom has a very shallow role, and that is mainly because I wanted to focus on the relationship between Ezra and his dad. However, in reality, my mother has played a dramatic role in my life and in helping me find my identity. She taught me how to become gentle and sweet. She also taught me sarcasm very well. Fathers understand the path of a young man better than mothers, but when it came to emotions, when it came to breakups or those times that I was being bullied, I much preferred my mother's comfort. She had a way of caring and loving me that made me feel safe and warm. I will forever be grateful for the unconditional love my mother continues to give me.

A Civil War Within started as a story for my son, as a way to help him learn from my story, but it turned into so much more. I am very proud of what is written on these pages. I hope that if just one person finds comfort in these words, all of this was worth the effort. This is my tamarisk tree.

www.ingramcontent.com/pod-product-compliance
Lightning Source LLC
Chambersburg PA
CBHW021158110726
47900CB00002B/629